**Shortlisted for the Blue Peter
'Book I Couldn't Put Down' Award**

'Johnson's writing is witty and inventive, and the character of Thora ... is full of unexpectedness ... This is a book full of fun.' *Sunday Times* children's book of the week

'Thora is an irresistible character with an attitude that's all her own! Though modern in its telling, this tale has a timeless feel to it – storytelling at its best.' Starred review, *Publishing News*

Thora

Thora

written and illustrated by
Gillian Johnson

Hodder
Children's
Books

A division of Hachette Children's Books

Text and illustrations copyright © 2003 Gillian Johnson

First published by HarperCollins Publishers,
Sydney, Australia, in 2003.
This edition published by arrangement with
HarperCollins Publishers Pty Limited.

This paperback edition published in Great Britain in 2005
by Hodder Children's Books

7

A Catalogue record for this book is available
from the British Library

ISBN-13: 9780340884140

Printed and bound in Great Britain by
Clays Ltd, St Ives plc

The paper and board used in this paperback by Hodder
Children's Books are natural recyclable products made from
wood grown in sustainable forests. The manufacturing
processes conform to the environmental regulations
of the country of origin.

Hodder Children's Books
A division of Hachette Children's Books
338 Euston Road, London NW1 3BH
An Hachette Livre UK company

For Ron Reichertz

Prologue

The trouble with humans
Is that their legs do not have scales
Their feet do not have flippers
Their heads don't blow like whales
Their swimming is atrocious
Their voices sound like rust
Their eyes are dimmed by air and often
Blinded by the dust.

The trouble with mermaids
Is that their tails do not have feet
Their fins do not have toes
And their legs are obsolete.
Their running is atrocious
Their voices sound like rain
Their eyes are dimmed by oceans
And they like to drink champagne.

This is what I told a mermaid
Who came to ask advice
(She'd fallen for
A man named Thor
And wondered at what price):

'Love between a mermaid
And a man without a tail
Will make you happy for a day
But then it has to fail.

'If you produce a child
Half of the land and sea
It will have to live in both
In order to be free.

'Ten years at sea! Ten years on land!
Between two worlds this girl must stand!
And if this doesn't come to be'
(I told her rather peevishly)
'The gods will then meet secretly
They'll roll their eyes
They'll sip their tea
And who knows what
They will agree
For that
We'll have
To wait
And see.'

tall trees

Beware of dog sign   Gus

church   vet

Pet sho

Viking statue

Police station

rock garden

shoe shop

canoe

where I met RICKY   BA

FISH shop

MAYOR'S office   MAIN STREE

BOAT HOUSES

Cul de Sa

PIER

Bored wal

TO THE ROCK

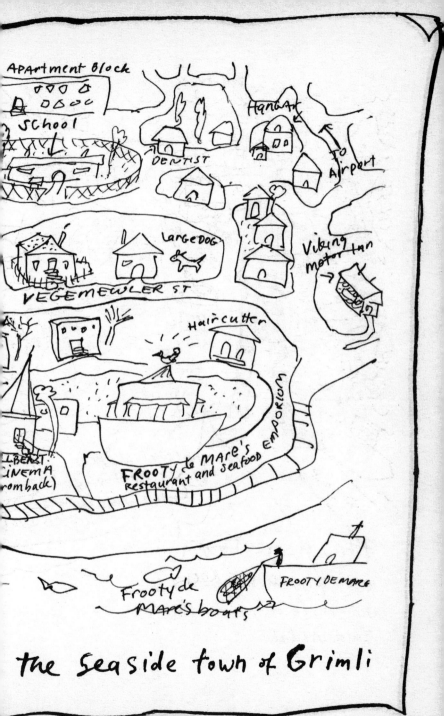

the Seaside town of Grimli

scrunchie
from chemist
in Swansea

clang

clang

windsurf slippers
(make satisfying
SMUCH SMUCH noise)

This is me, Thora,
wearing my HALLA SUIT
and three of my mother's
gold medals

Some people I know
plus 1 mermaid and
a peacock

blow hole

This beautiful lady with the
hair that smells like pumpkin pie
is my mother, Halla.

rain bonnet

And this is Cosmo, my pet peacock
from Flinders Island.

This very tall man is Mr. Walters
my Guardian Angle

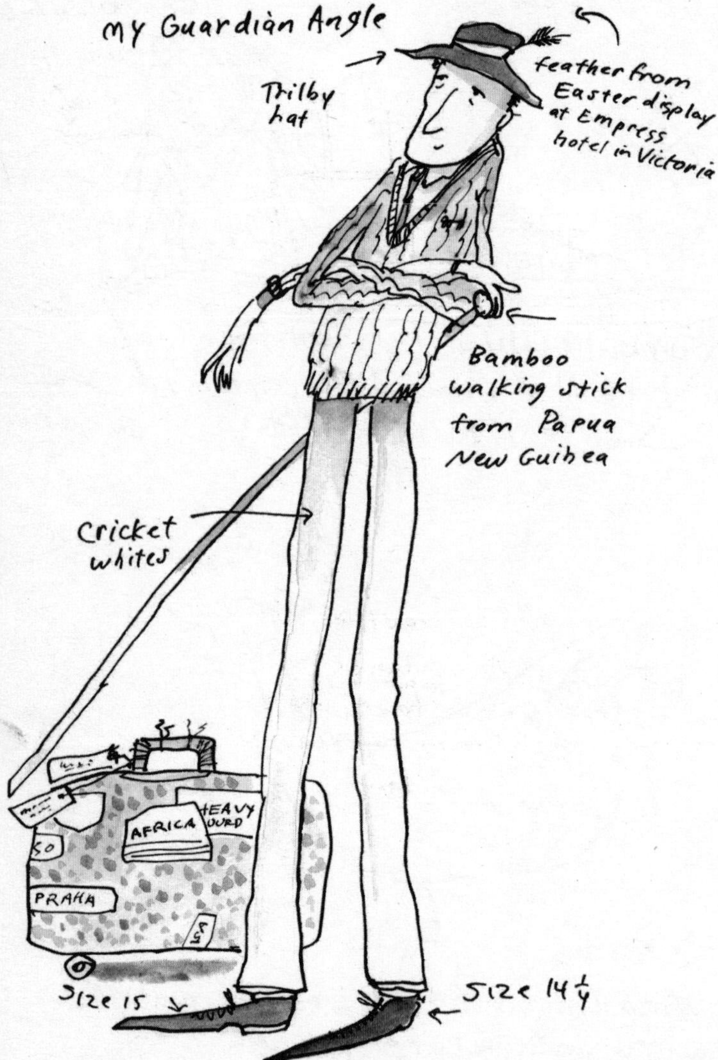

Trilby hat

feather from
Easter display
at Empress
hotel in Victoria

Bamboo
walking stick
from Papua
New Guinea

Cricket
whites

AFRICA HEAVY OURD

SO

PRAHA

SIZE 15   SIZE 14¼

TOGEther we all live on a small houseboat

OR at least we did
until we landed in a
small seaside town, GRIMLI,
to begin ten years of
life on land.

It was in Grimli
where I met

① HOLLY DE MARE

luxurious
curls

② RICKY RUKLE

Boiled
wool
from
Austria

can't swim →

Tiny
Stevens

③ Lynne

real patent leather

wants to
go to the
Moscow Circus →

LOTTIE   Flossie   DOTTIE

It's also where I <u>finally</u> met the Greenberg Sisters

Mr. Walters always said that you must never look over your shoulder or you'll turn into a pillar of sea salt. But sometimes you have to look back in order to go forward.....

Chapter 1

One fine summer evening a very tall man strolled along Grimli pier. He was not just tall, but very tall. He was so tall he could have been the president of the Tall Club. But he wasn't the president of anything any more. He was retired, and he was headed for the end of the pier, where he planned to sit on the red oil drum and smoke his last cigar of the evening.

He never made it.

With only a few steps to go, he heard a rather unusual cry. He stopped and scanned the harbour. Eventually, his eyes came to rest on the old houseboat with the FOR SALE sign. The *Loki*.

He'd noticed it before, but had never paused to take a good look. What made him take notice now was not the rather odd construction of the boat, nor the peeling paint of its cabin or even the crooked way it sat in the

water, but rather the loud noise coming out of it.

WAAAAAA! WAAAAAA! WAAAAAA!

He tiptoed over. The main glass window was steamed up and the curtains were drawn. Cupping his hand to his ear, he leaned his head against the front door and listened.

The crying was supernaturally loud.

It reminded him of all the worst things in life.

Dentist drills.

Cold showers.

Seasickness and creamed corn.

So why didn't he turn and run?

Mr Walters had never much liked babies, but this was different. The sheer volume of the crying reminded him of the effort of Olympic champions in some of the great photo finishes of his day. There was something heroic – noble even – in its amplitude. It made him want to join in.

He rapped on the cabin door. When nobody answered, he turned the metal handle and gently opened the door.

Not once did it occur to him not to.

The room was dark and damp and smelled distinctly fishy. When his eyes adjusted to the darkness, he gasped. 'Good gracious!'

Cut into the middle of the floor was a hole the size of an extra-large pepperoni pizza. The sea made a slurping sound as it splashed upwards. There were puddles everywhere.

On the walls, there were pictures of movie stars and posters advertising films. On the far side of the room stood a pile of dark furniture and a chest of drawers. The crying sound was coming from the opened bottom drawer. He rushed over.

WAAAAAA! WAAAAAA! WAAAAAA!

Tucked into a wad of wet green seaweed was a shrieking baby.

His first thought was that the creature must be very cold, because its rather scaly legs were quite purple.

He scooped it up. Immediately the crying stopped

and the baby opened one green eye. There was a click and a whooosh, and then a thin but powerful jet of water sprayed up and knocked his hat clear off his head. 'Ratbag!' he cried, stuffing the creature back into the drawer, where it resumed its crying, even harder and louder than before.

It was at that moment that Mr Walters noticed a hole on the top of the baby's bald head. It was no bigger than one of the foreign coins he tossed into wishing wells the world over.

'Deary me,' he whispered.

The baby kicked and thrashed.

WAAAAAAAA! WAAAAAA! WAAAAAA!

How could he get it to shut up? Should he sing it a song? He couldn't hold a tune.

Change its nappy? He didn't know how.

Hang the baby from the ceiling by its toes? What if it started to leak from the hole in its head?

Suddenly the baby reached up and grabbed his hand.

Mr Walters jumped back. Then he laughed. 'I know what you need,' he said. 'Won't be a minute ... you stay right where you are.'

WAAAAAAAAA!

Chapter 2

Many thousands of leagues below the *Loki*, Halla was making her way along the ocean floor to the home where she had grown up.

Two kilograms of fresh squid cheeks and an abalone shell filled with sea cucumber juice – Thora had refused it all.

Halla had been trying for days to feed her baby. Shark meat. Tuna. Crab's legs. A pudding of caviar and seal blubber. Nothing worked. Nothing stopped Thora's incessant cries. Halla was desperate. Neither child nor mother had slept for days.

Chapter 3

It was getting late and the shops in Grimli were closed, but a butter-coloured light shone in the windows of the Allbent Cinema. Three women, all sisters, were huddled around a blackboard. One of them was writing something. At the sound of a knock, they looked up, startled.

A very tall man peered in at them. He removed his hat and gave a sort of bow. 'Good evening,' he said through the glass.

The effect was courtly. One of the sisters, Flossie, judged the man a perfect gent. He had a manner and a voice right out of the movies. She trembled when she heard his English accent. Hadn't she seen him in something? She checked her pocket for a pen. She might ask him for his autograph.

'What do you want?' frowned Lottie, the tallest sister.

Dottie giggled nervously.

'I'm terribly sorry to disturb you,' he said, squinting up at the large clock on the wall, 'especially at this late hour ... but I wondered if you might ... I wonder if you have any milk for a baby?' He regarded them with surprised eyes, as if he didn't quite believe his own words. 'Yes,' he added hastily. 'The baby is very hungry and all the shops are closed.'

'Baby?'

'Yes.' He nodded politely.

The sisters looked relieved. They unlocked the doors and welcomed him in.

'Girl or boy?' asked Flossie.

Mr Walters had no idea. The image of the baby's face floated up before his eyes. 'Girl,' he guessed.

The sisters consulted each other. Then Dottie and Lottie excused themselves and went off to fetch some supplies.

Flossie smoothed her skirt. 'Is the baby your granddaughter?'

'In a manner of speaking,' he replied.

Flossie stared at him hard. 'Are you an actor, by any chance?' she asked.

'Good heavens no,' he replied.

'I feel I've seen you somewhere,' she said. 'Or *heard* you . . .'

'Really?' said Mr Walters. He looked over at the blackboard. Under the word BANISHED was a name. *Frooty de Mare.*

'An unfortunate appellation,' he said, changing the subject.

'It suits him,' replied Flossie.

At that moment, Dottie and Lottie returned carrying a large basket. It contained a bottle of milk, a thermos filled with extra milk (warmed to just the right temperature), a soft grey and yellow blanket, an ancient-looking blue bunny rabbit with a bell around its neck, and finally, a silver rattle in the shape of a dumbbell.

Mr Walters could not be sure, but he thought he saw tears in Dottie's eyes as she explained how to use the glass bottle. 'Everything is plastic now,' she said, 'but these old bottles are much nicer to drink from. My son used them over twenty years ago.'

'Dottie can't throw anything away,' said Flossie.

'Are you sure it's all right?' asked Mr Walters.

'Yes,' sniffed Dottie. 'The time has come.'

The two others nodded. They wished him and the little one well. Then Flossie walked him to the door.

'Hope we see you again,' she said with a wink.

Blushing, Mr Walters hurried back to the *Loki*.

Chapter 4

Halla paused at the front of her childhood home before swimming around to the back entrance. A window was open. She found her mother and grandmother in the living room.

'Can't help you,' said her mother coldly. She pressed a button on the wall. An alarm sounded.

Her grandmother buried her face in her hands and rocked in her rocking chair.

Her father swam into the room. 'What's going on in here?' When he saw his daughter, he narrowed his eyes. 'I HAVE NO DAUGHTER! TAKE HER AWAY!'

A reluctant sea-horse guard showed her the way out and slammed the gate in her face.

All of her old friends had swum the other way when they saw her.

All but her best friend.

Marina required no explanation. She took Halla's hand. 'The Sea Shrew might help you.'

Chapter 5

The baby was still howling. Mr Walters stooped over her basket. With a nervous hand, he tilted the bottle up and placed the rubber teat in her mouth. A little bit of milk dribbled out but her eyes clamped shut and she latched on. Silence.

'Good girl,' whispered Mr Walters. 'You *are* a girl?'

While she drank, Mr Walters folded the blanket and draped it over the edge of the drawer. He tucked the bunny rabbit next to her. He set the extra milk on the kitchen counter. Then he lit a cigar and pushed a chair up beside the baby to sit and watch.

When she had drained the bottle, she opened her eyes and belched.

In that instant, Mr Walters felt his heart spring open. And before he could shut it again, the little baby with the supernatural cry, the violet legs and the hole in her head the size of an Icelandic króna climbed into it and fell asleep. On her face was a look of utter contentment.

The rummy cigar smoke swirled through the room.

Mr Walters had not realised until that moment how lonely his life had been. For the first time in many years, he felt happy.

13

chapter 6

The Sea-Shrew rolled her eyes when she saw Halla.

'I knew I would see you again, you numbskull. Marrying a human! Well, he's gone now, isn't he? And you're left with a half-human child. Did you expect it to work out differently?'

Halla looked down at her tail. 'I don't know what to do. The baby's been crying for five days.'

'I know. I can hear her. It's obnoxious!'

'How do I get her to stop?'

'Feed her!'

'She won't take my milk. I think it might be too salty.'

'Give her human food, you idiot!'

Halla ignored the old woman's taunts. 'How do I raise a half-human child? Please! I have no idea what to do!'

'You want practical advice? Go to your mother.' The Shrew ran her fingers through her wiry grey hair. 'I talk destiny.'

'What *is* her destiny?' asked Marina quickly.

The Sea Shrew sat very still and closed her eyes. Then in a superior voice she began to speak. *'If she can live between worlds for ten years, this daughter of hers can live. Otherwise, mother and daughter will go the way of the human husband.'*

Marina squeezed Halla's hand. 'What happened to him?'

Halla shook her head. 'Don't know,' she whispered.

The old hag grinned enigmatically. 'Unions between humans and mermaids are forbidden, Halla, you knew that. Now you must pay. Very few can live between worlds. On your daughter's tenth birthday, you must deliver her back to the land. To the world of her father. *If she lives that long.'*

If mermaids could cry, Halla would have flooded the seas.

'How fascinating,' said the Sea Shrew suddenly, gazing upward.

'What?' asked Halla.

'Your daughter has stopped crying.'

The Shrew's words did not reassure Halla. Nervously, she thanked the old hag.

'Don't be upset,' said Marina, as they swam off. 'She's a nasty old drama queen.'

Halla gave her friend a hug and headed back to the World Above.

To the *Loki*.

And to her newborn baby, Thora.

chapter 7

The first thing Halla noticed as she swam up towards the *Loki* was the silence.

It was like the quiet at the bottom of the Marianas Trench.

She swam as fast as she could, a creeping chill in the pit of her stomach. No matter how much sea water she gulped, her throat felt dry.

How could she *possibly* feed her child human food? Where would it come from? How? It was all *impossible!*

It seemed to take forever, but finally she surfaced in the harbour and slipped silently under the *Loki*.

The cigar smoke confused her. She wondered for an instant if she had surfaced in the wrong boat.

But no.

She raised herself up on her arms and peered over at her child.

Thora's cheeks were pink. Her eyes closed. There was a smile on her lips.

The regular little breaths were the sweetest music Halla had ever heard.

'My dear woman,' came a human voice through the smoke.

A vision in white. Like a ghost. A very tall, very thin ghost.

'Can I give you a hand?'

He had a kindly, creased face with a long, hooked nose.

'Mr Jack Walters,' he whispered, extending his hand. 'I heard your baby crying ... I assume it is yours? Yes? Good. Girl? Yes. Good. I couldn't help but worry. Oh, dear. Now *you* look worried. Don't be scared. I am very sorry for trespassing. I don't know what came over me! I'll leave immediately. I was just concerned that this little baby ... your child, that is ... seemed hungry, hungry enough to eat my hand.'

His eyes fell on Halla's tail. 'Good gracious me!'

Not for the first time that evening, Mr Walters gaped. His eyes nearly popped out of their sockets.

'Buying the boat, are you?' she asked sadly.

'Nooooo.' Mr Walters shook his head, his eyes still fastened on her tail.

She believed him. 'Never seen a mermaid?'

'No.'

'Well, you have now.' Halla motioned to the baby. 'How did you get her to sleep?'

'Milk.'

'What sort?'

Mr Walters looked worried. 'I'm not entirely sure,' he said. 'Is there more than one sort? I'm not very experienced at this sort of thing. I suppose it's cow's milk.' He held up the thermos. 'There's more right here.'

Human food. 'Thank you.' Halla rested on her arms, tail in the water. She closed her eyes. 'Sorry to be rude, but I'm very tired.'

As she drifted off to sleep, she sensed him slipping a pillow under her head. She heard the words 'pumpkin pie'. The creak of floorboards. The click of a door.

Chapter 8

What on earth would happen to the mermaid and her baby?

This was the question Mr Walters pondered the next morning as he ironed his cricket whites. He liked his trousers to keep their crease and so he travelled with a little portable electric iron.

In his rather long life, Mr Walters had, as they say, done it all. Sailor, swimmer, coach, poet, journalist, sports official, cricket commentator. He'd fought in a war and he'd tried to write a novel. Now that he was retired, he spent his time travelling around the world. And he liked to stay in small inns in out-of-the-way seaside towns where nobody recognised him. Where he could read and smoke his cigars without people hounding him for his autograph.

When he was dressed and packed, he called a taxi

cab and carried his bags down the steep stairs of the Blue Bell Bed and Breakfast.

His holiday in Grimli was over.

'I've had a *marvellous* time,' he said to Mrs Valihora, the owner. 'See you next year.'

'You won't be staying *here*, Mr Walters,' she said. She set her mop against the wall and took his keys.

'What is it?' he asked. 'Have I offended you?'

'No, no.' Then Mrs Valihora informed Mr Walters that the Blue Bell was about to be knocked down. 'The wrecking ball will be paying us a visit some time next month.'

'How terrible!' said Mr Walters.

'Yes. I would have told you sooner, but I didn't want to spoil your holiday.'

Mr Walters looked through the window at the crashing surf. Not far off, bobbing in the harbour, he could see the *Loki*.

The image of the little baby floated up in his mind, as if on a screen.

Would she and her mother be safe?

'There's nothing to be done,' Mrs Valihora continued.

'Why?'

'Ask Frooty de Mare,' she said.

Mr Walters recalled the blackboard at the cinema. 'Who is he exactly?'

'Some call him an entrepreneur. I call him a *shark*. He's buying up all the sea-front property. He wants to put us all out of business.'

'What is he going to build?'

'He wants to flatten the cinema and replace it with a big, ugly hotel.'

Mr Walters shuddered. 'Dreadful.'

'But there's a fly in the ointment.'

'What's that?'

'The Greenberg sisters won't sell.'

'Why not?'

Mrs Valihora smiled. 'I figure they love the movies too much.'

The old journalist in him nodded. 'So how do you explain Frooty's ambition?'

'You see, Frooty's father left when he was very young, and Frooty and his mother suffered. They both had to go out to work. Frooty worked harder than anyone I've ever seen, I'll hand him that – but there was something warped about his drive. He proved himself, but it wasn't enough. Now he wants to buy up the whole town!'

'But how could he afford to do that?'

'Fishing. He owns the fleets. This is a poor town. People want cash and he's got it.'

There was a honk.

'There's your cab,' said Mrs Valihora.

Mr Walters tipped his hat, and as he carried out his bags his gaze once again fell on the *Loki*. He imagined a wrecking ball smashing it to bits. A flicker of anger cleared his mind. He had an idea.

Chapter 9

'Airport?' said the cab driver.

'Not yet,' said Mr Walters. 'I want to stop first at the pier. The *Loki*. Do you know it?'

'Sure,' said the driver. 'It's an old houseboat that used to belong to a local lad. He disappeared without a trace last Christmas.'

'How terrible!' exclaimed Mr Walters. 'What happened to him?'

'You ask a lot of questions. You one of those private detectives or something?'

'Just curious.'

'There're lots of different theories about what might have happened.' The cab driver pressed a button. Water squirted out on to the windscreen. Then he switched on the wipers. 'One theory was that he eloped. Another was that he was travelling the world.' He shook his head. 'Then there're the stories that you wouldn't believe.'

'Such as?'

'You'll think I'm on my way to the funny farm.'

'Come on, dear chap.'

The driver shrugged. 'I heard that he'd fallen for a mermaid.'

Mr Walters felt his heart skip a beat. 'Yes?'

'Probably a lot of rubbish. But these stories spring up when a person disappears. Anyway, I've heard Frooty de Mare is going to buy the *Loki* – if he hasn't already.'

'Why does Frooty de Mare want the boat?'

'He doesn't want the *boat* – it's worth diddly-squat. He wants the lease on the *berth*. If he owns that lease, then he owns the entire harbour, because he's already bought all the other leases. Next to the cinema, this is the most valuable real estate in town. Anyway, no drama really. He's probably the only one in town who can pay cash for it. Money talks. I'm telling you, I picked the wrong profession.'

In the back seat of the cab, Mr Walters felt the way he had when the Greek cheat Stavros Constaninopolis won an Olympic medal he didn't deserve.

'If I wanted to buy the *Loki* and its lease, where would I go?'

'Seriously?'

'Yes.'

The car did a U-turn. Tyres squealing, the taxi headed back to the centre of town and pulled up beside a building and a large hand-painted sign.

chapter 10

Halla nearly jumped out of her scales.

RAP! RAP! RAP!

The FOR SALE sign had been  posted by the harbour authorities a few months before Thora's birth.

The rules were clear. If the dues weren't paid, the boat had to be sold.

From the water, she'd seen the houseboat-hunters come and go. Jolly folk in sunglasses and deck shoes. Once she'd returned to find the furniture pushed against the wall. The fridge cleaned out. The windows polished. She had no way of knowing when they were coming, or how long they'd stay. Usually they didn't even knock.

Halla slipped the baby into her bed and pushed the bottom drawer three-quarters shut.

Immediately, Thora began to cry.

'Drat,' whispered Halla.

RAP! RAP! RAP!

She scooped Thora out of her seaweed bed and held her tight. 'Shhhh,' she whispered in her ear. She was about to slip into the water when she smelled the spicy cigar smoke from the night before. Her heart lifted. 'Mr Walters?' she asked cautiously.

The door opened. In the crack of light, she saw the vision in white. The kindly creased face. The long nose. He reminded Halla of the enormous, majestic sea horses that guarded the castle where she had grown up at the bottom of the sea, back when she was welcome in her parents' home.

Thora had stopped crying, and regarded Mr Walters with wide eyes and a broad, toothless smile.

'Sorry to bother you again, my dear woman, but I've been giving your situation some thought.' He rattled a set of keys. 'I just bought the *Loki*. I wondered if we might have a chat?'

chapter 11

Once again, Mr Walters asked Halla to repeat, word for word, what the Sea Shrew had said.

They spoke in whispers so as not to wake the sleeping baby.

This time, he wrote it down in a small notebook that he used to record cricket scores.

If she can live between worlds for ten years, this daughter of hers can live. Otherwise, mother and daughter will go the way of the human husband.

Mr Walters lit a cigar and let the words swirl around him.

Halla rested on her elbows, her tail in the water. The words 'live between worlds' had become a riddle. A riddle that was much more difficult than the cryptic crossword in the *Daily Seasider* which Thor had said that he loved to solve.

As Mr Walters had said, buying the *Loki* was only the first step.

'Now explain to me how you got here,' said Mr Walters gently.

'Ever since I can remember,' said Halla, 'I wanted to visit the World Above. My parents were against it. I did it anyway. On my way up, I ran into trouble. I got tangled up in some human garbage, an old plastic bag. Somehow I surfaced and made my way to the Rock.'

She pointed to the large black rock three or four kilometres out from the harbour. Mr Walters, who was a little short-sighted, squinted out to sea and nodded.

'On my way there I felt a sharp pain in my tail, right about here.' She pointed to a silvery patch where her scales were a lighter colour. 'I'd been hooked by a fisherman. The fisherman was Thor, out for a relaxing evening of fishing after a long shift at the cinema, where he worked as the projectionist. He told me to return home. To go back where I came from. He was so upset by the injury he'd caused me, and he had such an enchanting smile and a gentle way about him that I couldn't bear to leave him. I knew the dangers and so did he. But we fell head over tails over feet in love anyway. He said my hair smelled of pumpkin pie. He was the most poetic creature I'd ever met. But five days after we married, he disappeared.'

'You've heard nothing since?'

'Not a word.'

'Terrible,' said Mr Walters.

'Yes,' blinked Halla. 'I lived in and around the boat for the next nine months. I was too frightened to think straight. I just let myself float along, hoping I would come up with some sort of plan. But time passes quickly when you're not in a rush.'

Mr Walters nodded. He had spent most of his life worrying about the time. On one arm alone he wore four wristwatches so he could know at a glance the time in London, Brisbane, Rome and Winnipeg.

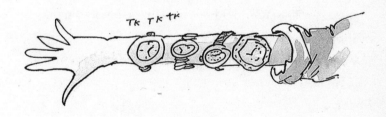

'Thora was born a week ago.' Halla let her hair fall into her eyes so he could not see her distress. 'I love her more than anything and yet I don't know how to raise her.'

Truth was, Mr Walters was a little worried too. For one thing, he had spent most of his retirement savings on the boat and its lease. Furthermore, he was supposed to be attending the Wimbledon finals right now. He would be missing some *cracking* good tennis.

Over in her bed of seaweed, little Thora stirred. Mr Walters felt a smile on his lips. Fate had led him here, to this town, to this boat, and it was too late to turn back.

Clearly, it was meant to be.

'Halla,' he said, a little awkwardly. 'Everything is going to be all right.' As he said it, he believed it. For the first time he was not the journalist, or the cricket commentator, or the swimming official. He was what he was. A retired old geezer with time on his hands and the desire to help a mermaid in distress. They had a place to live. Now they needed money to live on. None of this did he mention to Halla. Not yet, anyway. 'The World Above will be a lot less murky after a good night's sleep.'

Halla frowned slightly, but she nodded. 'Sleep is a good idea.'

Chapter 12

Frooty de Mare was gobsmacked when he learned that the *Loki* and its ninety-nine year lease had been sold right under his great big nose!

He paced up and down the corridor in the estate agent's office grilling the poor estate agent. This was the first time in years that anybody outside Grimli had bought a property. People from elsewhere simply didn't *do* that. He couldn't believe it. 'What was the shyster's name?'

'He called himself Walters.'

'Why didn't you let me know?'

'I hadn't heard from you in *five months*. I sent you letters asking you to get moving on it and didn't hear back. I figured you'd moved on to bigger and better things.'

'I can't move on to bigger and better things without this lease. I can't develop this two-bit harbour unless I own *each* and *every* berth. I have a lot of money riding on this project. Big money. Bigger money than you'll ever know about. *I'm in the big leagues, buster.* I'm playing the high-power real estate game. And you . . .'

Terror flashed in the poor agent's eyes. 'He paid in cash.'

'I don't care if he paid in gold. I need that lease!'

Chapter 13

The next morning Mr Walters sat on a deck chair watching Halla swim circles in the harbour with her infant daughter in her arms. She was swimming so fast that Mr Walters grew dizzy. Suddenly, it came to him – an idea so perfect, so practical, and so *possible*, that he began to laugh. He retrieved his stopwatch from his bag and waved at Halla to come over.

'How long might it take you to swim to shore and back again?'

Halla shrugged. 'Not sure.'

She handed Thora over to Mr Walters and set off. In no time at all, she was back again.

'Extraordinary,' said Mr Walters.

She was not even out of breath!

'What about to the Rock?'

For Halla, it was an amusing game. She grinned and pushed off. He watched her glide through the water,

the power of her tail propelling her soundlessly as a
seal, her arms reaching gracefully as if she were
saluting starfish on a summer's day.

Yes, Halla reminded Mr Walters of the great open-
water swimmer Marcella von Ditz. The only female to
cross the Great Gonzo River in Mexico, the Bermuda
Triangle and Bass Strait. He had reported all three
achievements on the BBC.

It took Halla less than ten minutes to swim to the
Rock and back again. 'A world record,' whispered Mr
Walters into Thora's ear. 'Without a doubt.'

'I say, my dear, have you ever considered
competitive swimming?'

'What's that?' asked Halla.

Mr Walters explained.

He told Halla that swimming had a long and
honourable human history.

'People *love* water. They bathe, shower, swim, dive,
boat, float, race. They compete in swimming pools for

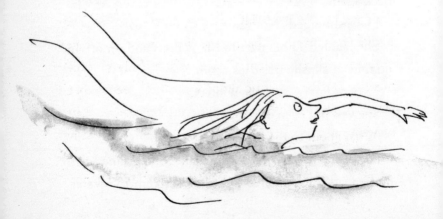

medals and ribbons and silver trays and pen sets and professional sponsorships. They also swim down rivers, across lakes and seas. They've always done it. They probably always will.'

Halla was amazed. 'You're telling me that humans actually swim across lakes and seas for *money*?'

Mr Walters tried to consider the idea from a mermaid's point of view. 'Perhaps it seems a little ... well, silly, to you ... but yes, it is not uncommon for a talented swimmer to live very comfortably off their winnings.'

Halla looked a little overcome. 'It's tragic, really,' she said.

'What do you mean?' said Mr Walters.

'Human beings are so badly designed for water.' She held up her hand. 'No webbing. No gills. And legs must be a dreadful burden. My husband told me that humans have to hold their breath or else they'll drown.'

'Well, yes.'

'Once I saw some people swimming on the sea floor with CLUB ATLANTIC written on their suits. Thor said they were scuba divers. They were so loaded down with equipment – face masks, tanks on their backs and long plastic flippers on their feet – that I couldn't see how they were enjoying themselves. They swam off when they saw me.' She looked down at her tail and sighed. 'Then again, I suppose I'm not very well designed for land.'

'No,' agreed Mr Walters. 'But your child is. And our challenge is for you and Thora to live not on land, but *between worlds*. To be of both land and water. Swimming races might be just the ticket.'

'It seems too easy.'

'Easy?' said Mr Walters. 'Nothing worth doing is easy. You will have to hide your tail. Adapt to different water temperatures. Find ways to persuade people you are human. Also, it won't always be easy for Thora. It will mean constant travel. She will have to live on the *Loki*. Speak different languages. Adapt. But I will be able to help. I know a fair amount about the way these competitions are run. I'll be the middleman. And as Thora's guardian grandfather, I can take care of the human side of things.'

'They really give *prize money* for swimming down a river? It just sounds so far-fetched.'

'Does that mean you'll give it a try?'

'I'd be crazy not to.'

That evening, Mr Walters made some telephone calls to his friends around the world. In the morning he handed Halla a list of open-water competitions. 'The prize money is very good these days!'

There was no time to waste. The open-water swimming season was already underway. The first race was to be held on the Thames.

The odd little family set sail in the *Loki* immediately.

Chapter 14

Frooty de Mare took a deep breath of clean, crisp Grimli air.

He would bottle it and call it 'Champagne by the Sea'. Sell it for $20 a pop. Frooty prided himself on his good ideas. He considered himself a genius.

Meanwhile, he needed to sort out this *Loki* business. He would act like a professional. He would stay calm. The best businessmen didn't lose their tempers, although sometimes geniuses did.

These were his thoughts as he headed by foot to the *Loki* to have a little chat with this Walters character.

He paused to survey the coastline. He felt like an artist facing a big blank canvas, poised to paint his masterpiece. In a few weeks' time, construction would begin on the Tooty Frooty Hotel and Seafood Emporium. This boring stretch of coastline would be transformed into a snazzy seaside restaurant for discriminating holiday-goers with cash in their pockets. Once he got his hands on the cinema's prime real estate, he'd start construction on the Fun House, a five-star hotel with a revolving restaurant and vibrating octopus-shaped beds. Then there were the plans for the harbour. He had the name: *De Mare's Magnificent Marina*. Yes, there was no shortage of good ideas.

He just needed to solve this little glitch with the *Loki*.

But when he got there, the *Loki* was gone.

Chapter 15

Mr Walters cradled the howling Thora in the *Loki* as Halla swam and won the race down the Thames.

The crowds loved her. Even the competitors she'd beaten loved her. Her modesty appealed to everyone. She didn't wear make-up or act flash. She spoke in a quaint style with an accent that nobody was able to place. When asked where she was from, she merely shrugged and said, 'The bottom of the sea. Why?' That response seemed to drive everybody wild. The television interview with the BBC went very well. Nobody found it odd that Halla insisted on speaking to the reporters from the pizza-shaped hole in the floor of the *Loki*.

'How are you going to celebrate tonight, Halla?'

'I think I'll make an octopus-cheek casserole and perhaps a little later I'll take my daughter, Thora, for a swim.'

Her face appeared on the cover of a number of magazines. It probably didn't hurt that she was, as the newspaper reporters kept pointing out, 'rather photogenic'. Her eyes were large and grey and her hair was blonde and smelled faintly of pumpkin pie. Even those people who don't like the taste of pumpkin pie, or its damp and mushy texture, admit that it has a delicious smell.

After the success of her Thames swim, Halla was immediately invited to swim some of the great lakes of the world. She swam Lake Baikal in Russia. Then Lake Lagoda by the Gulf of Finland and Lake Titicaca in Peru. She was invited to swim the Dead Sea, but the high salt content bothered her eyes so she swam the Danube instead.

To escape the beady eyes of the officials, Halla wore a special mermaid-disguising wetsuit. Mr Walters had it flown in specially for her swim across Lake Geneva. Inspired by the swimming greats Esther Williams and Annette Kellerman, it gave the illusion of two legs. At the same time, it directed attention to Halla's very human-looking upper body. Dubbed 'The Halla-Skin', it very quickly became a fashion item and was sold in beach and boating shops around the world. A child-size suit was made for Thora. She had started to swim by then and her Halla-Skin kept her very warm in the cold water.

Frooty de Mare
PO Box 100
Grimli-By-The-Sea
18 November

Dear Mr Walters,

Let me introduce myself. My name is Frooty de
Mare, CEO of Tooty Frooty Enterprises, Grimli. No
doubt you have heard of me. I am what you might
call 'a big fish in a small pond' – a successful and
prosperous force in the community, a role model for
the young, an inspiration for the old.

It has come to my attention that you are now the
proud owner of the *Loki*. First, let me congratulate
you on your recent purchase. I am sure you will
enjoy many hours of sailing pleasure.

Now, might I address a small point? Given that
you have chosen an exciting life abroad, you will
surely have no use for the *Loki*'s ninety-nine year
lease. In fact, I am certain that it is a burden for
you to own something so far away and so utterly
useless to you in any practical way.

I would like, therefore, to release you from this tiresome obligation and offer to transfer the lease into my own name. I will assume all responsibility from hence on. You need only sign the attached form in the space indicated. No witness required. I humbly offer this service Free of Charge. (No messy paperwork! No processing fee!)

Again, my very best to you. Please find, for your convenience, a self-addressed envelope enclosed.

Sincerely,
Frooty de Mare.

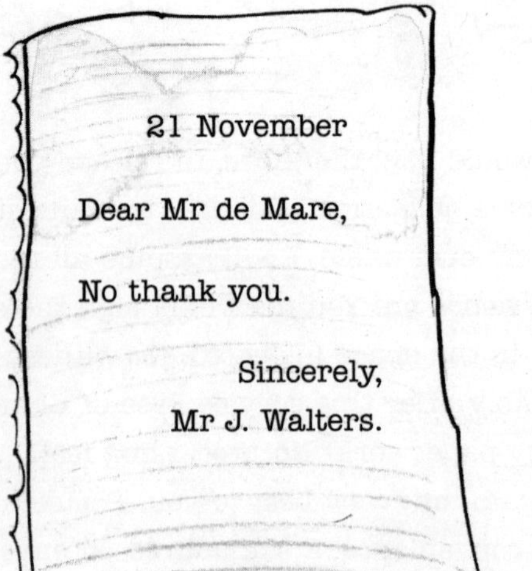

21 November

Dear Mr de Mare,

No thank you.

　　　Sincerely,
　Mr J. Walters.

Chapter 16

Within a few years, Halla was known in the open-water swimming world as 'Halla's Comet'. She rarely appeared to be tired and was never cold. The jellyfish did not sting her. The sharks treated her respectfully. She had a superb swimming style and a unique splashless kick. She won dozens of gold medals and earned thousands of pounds. The *Loki* slowly filled with interesting and unique gifts and prizes – diamond-studded goggles from Zurich, gold-plated flippers, a tortoiseshell table, thirteen pen sets and twenty-one silver trays.

The most beloved prize of all was a blue-necked Indian peacock named Cosmo from Flinders Island. Cosmo was Thora's constant companion, and, along with Mr Walters, the three of them always sailed in the *Loki* alongside Halla as she swam.

Sometimes the races were very long and boring. Thora loved to dangle over the side of the boat and

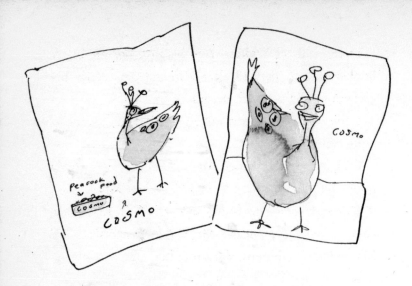

talk to her mother. Sometimes she read stories to her from one of the books that Mr Walters kept in constant supply – *The Red Book of Dogs, Treasure Island, A Field Guide to Tasmanian Birds, The Water Babies.*

'Mother!' she shouted as Halla swam the Coral Sea near Vanuatu. 'Did you know that a Tasmanian Devil can chew through bone?'

In Savu Savu, Fiji, she developed an interest in polar bears. 'Hollow fur!' And in Martinique she worried about the rabbits she'd seen aboard the Finnish yacht *Bad Weather.* 'If they eat tomatoes, they could die!'

Thora's reading and chatter kept Halla awake as she tackled the rivers and lakes of the world.

When Thora was five she was caught drawing a duck-billed platypus on a clean, pressed pair of Mr Walters' cricket whites.

'Here,' said Mr Walters. And he gave her the blank book in which he had always intended to write his great novel. 'Draw your pictures in this.'

'I don't want to write a novel,' said Thora, 'I want to write and draw my *life*.'

'Excellent plan,' clapped Mr Walters. 'I always prefer books with pictures.'

Thora opened the book and stared at the blank page. Then with one of Mr Walters' special Josiah Mason Fine Point pens, she wrote her name.

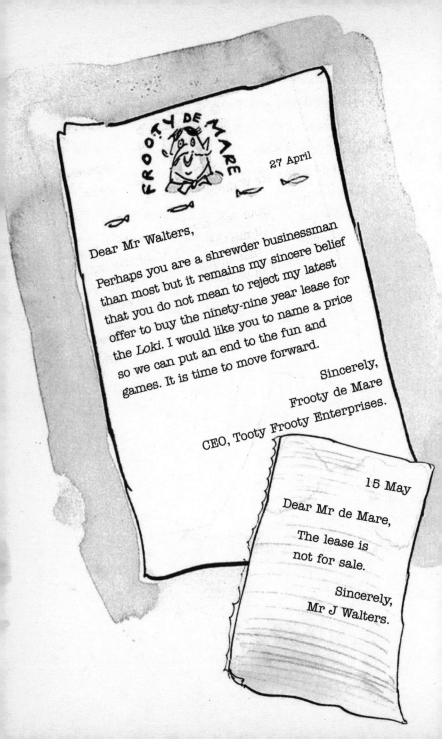

FROOTY DE MARE

27 April

Dear Mr Walters,

Perhaps you are a shrewder businessman than most but it remains my sincere belief that you do not mean to reject my latest offer to buy the ninety-nine year lease for the *Loki*. I would like you to name a price so we can put an end to the fun and games. It is time to move forward.

Sincerely,
Frooty de Mare
CEO, Tooty Frooty Enterprises.

15 May

Dear Mr de Mare,

The lease is not for sale.

Sincerely,
Mr J Walters.

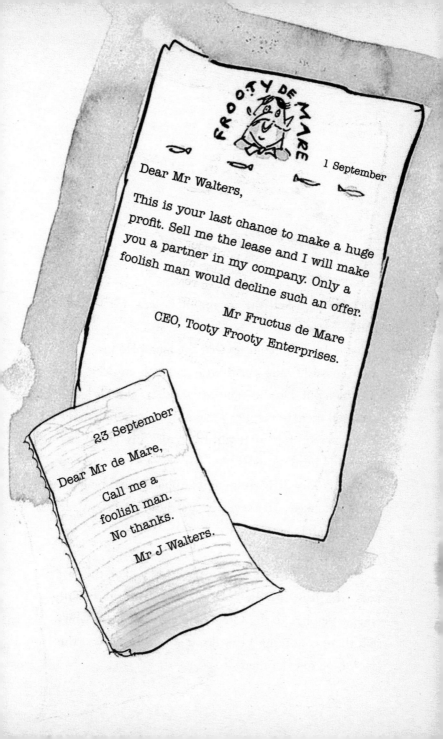

FROOTY DE MARE

1 September

Dear Mr Walters,

This is your last chance to make a huge profit. Sell me the lease and I will make you a partner in my company. Only a foolish man would decline such an offer.

Mr Fructus de Mare
CEO, Tooty Frooty Enterprises.

23 September

Dear Mr de Mare,

Call me a
foolish man.
No thanks.

Mr J Walters.

Chapter 17

'Evict them?' asked the mayor of Grimli, Mr Grimus Grubb. 'How?'

'Just tell the Greenbergs that the land belongs to the town council, issue them with eviction notices, and kick them out. Do the same with Walters and his lease. Then sell them to me. I can make you a very rich man.'

The mayor folded his arms across his chest and shook his head. 'Impossible.' For seven years, he had granted Frooty de Mare permits to build what he liked where he liked. For seven years, he'd let Frooty de Mare push him around.

No more.

'My hands are bound,' he said firmly. 'For the last time, the lease to the *Loki* belongs to Walters. The cinema belongs to the Greenberg sisters. If they won't sell, there is nothing I can do. It would be against the law for me to evict them.'

'So?'

'I can't do it.'

'You mean you *won't* do it.'

The two men glared at each other.

Then Frooty looked out the vast office window at the sodium-orange neon glow from the Tooty Frooty Hotel and Seafood Restaurant, now seven years old. 'Meany,' he glowered.

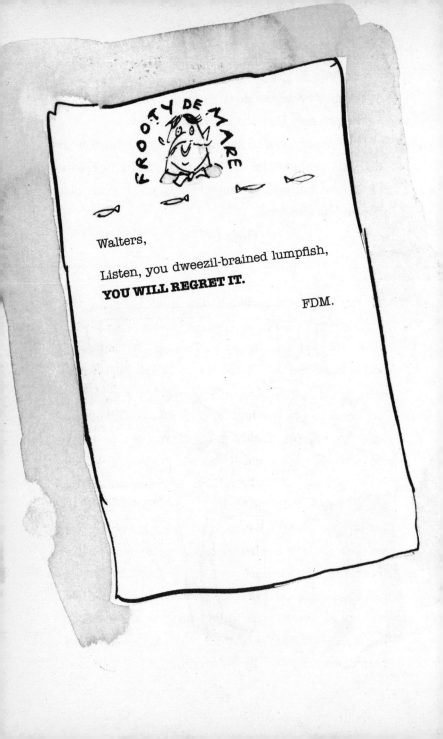

FROOTY DE MARE

Walters,

Listen, you dweezil-brained lumpfish,
YOU WILL REGRET IT.

FDM.

chapter 18

By the time her mother had crossed Lake Balcash, 480 kilometres from the Chinese border, Thora could walk, talk, somersault, say hello in twelve languages and hoist a sail. Mr Walters had taught her to play cricket. He had taught her how to ride a bicycle. He had even taught her how to cook. Before her eighth birthday, Thora could make Thai chicken satay, Ukrainian perogies and Italian spaghetti. Mr Walters was a good coach and a reliable human guardian. He treated Thora like his own grandchild. In time, he couldn't imagine life without her. Sometimes he had to go off to attend to what he called his 'kitchen of life'. But he always came back.

And as he grew older, it was Thora who used her two young legs to walk to the shops to buy the milk, her scales well hidden beneath her Halla-Skin and her purple feet covered by windsurfing slippers. It was

Thora who collected Halla's prizes on behalf of her mother, Thora who finally reminded everybody that after the next major swim they would have to head back to Grimli, because their ten years between worlds was almost up.

As the Sea Shrew said
   If you produce a child
   Half of the land and sea
   It will have to live in both
   In order to be Free

TEN YEARS AT SEA! TEN YEARS ON LAND!
BETWEEN TWO WORLDS THIS GIRL MUST STAND!

Prophecies are always a little
confusing but it doesn't take a
~~brain surgeon~~ circumpolar navigation
officer to understand that I had
to get myself to land.

   What better place to go than to
   where daddy grew up?

Chapter 19

On the eve of Thora's tenth birthday, Thora, Halla, Mr Walters and Cosmo set sail for Grimli. Passage through the Panama Canal and the Pacific and Indian Oceans was rough. The *Loki* took a beating, and though they made good time the vessel was leaking by the time they reached the Rock.

Mr Walters was pitched into gloom. They would have to find a place to stay until the boat was repaired. 'I hadn't planned for this,' he fussed. 'Life can be so trying sometimes.'

Thora was gloomy too, but for different reasons. The Rock, situated three or four kilometres from town, was to be Halla's new home. 'You've got to be kidding ... you're actually going to live *here*?'

'Yes,' sang Halla. 'Isn't it wonderful?' She greeted it like an old friend. She seemed familiar with every fissure. It was full of 'potential', she said, and had a number of 'terrific lounging opportunities'.

Thora did not think the Rock was wonderful. *At all.*

It was the size of a squash court, though oblong in shape, and hedged with pebbly bits and tooth-shaped rocks. Flattish. A sloping ramp at the north end that was furred with mosses, lichens, seaweed. It just sat there doing nothing. It was just a boring old rock.

To Mr Walters, it looked like a Stilton cheese after a large dinner party. Maybe a month after. Gone off. Briny smelling.

But Cosmo seemed to sense that it was alive with hundreds of tiny sea creatures. He fanned his tail and held his beak up to catch the fishy smells.

'Look,' said Halla, 'I know it's not exactly luxury accommodation. But I'm a mermaid, remember? I don't need roofs and beds and hairdryers and television sets. The wind will be my hairdryer and the sea will be my fridge.'

'It doesn't even have a toilet,' said Thora.

They all surveyed the Rock in silence.

'Well,' said Mr Walters suddenly, 'here's a plus. The view is excellent. You can see the Grimli pier from here.'

'Exactly,' said Halla. She began unpacking her bags. 'What are you all waiting for? We have a birthday party to celebrate!'

They all set to scrubbing away the slime with pumice stones. Halla braided the slippery bits of

seaweed and shook out an old red and white
chequered tablecloth. Then she produced Thora's
favourite – pineapple sea-foam angel cake.

It was a bittersweet occasion.

Mr Walters smoked his cigar and stared at a distant
point on the sea.

Cosmo scratched at the lichen with his three
pointed toes.

Halla busied herself cleaning up and settling in.

Thora tried to imagine the life that lay ahead.

Soon, Mr Walters and Cosmo sailed off in the *Loki*
to make arrangements. In a few hours, they would
collect Thora and take her to Grimli to begin her life
on land.

chapter 20

Mother and daughter were alone together.

With a comb made of abalone shell, Halla brushed Thora's hair as she had done since Thora was small. She fastened it in a ponytail at the top of her head. 'You've got to hide your blow hole. Humans don't spout water out of the tops of their heads and they'll find it strange.'

She handed Thora a bag containing two wetsuits. 'The scales on your legs are beautiful, but sadly, humans find them ugly. You just can't risk it. I've heard of a mermaid who was de-scaled by humans. She died. Be very, very careful. Keep them covered at all times. As for the puddles from your blow hole, they'll assume you've wet yourself. Humans always take the silliest position on this sort of thing. Always carry something to mop up.'

Finally, she pushed a rusted pewter tea chest toward Thora. It had been awarded to Halla in China after she'd swum the River Xi.

'Humans are creatures of custom. Always take a present when you visit. Afterwards, write a thank you note. People consider you quite rude otherwise. And try not to make yourself too conspicuous. Be very careful about who you get to know. If you run into any sort of trouble, go to the movies. Your father once worked at the Allbent Cinema. And never forget that the sisters saved your life when you were one week old.'

Thora nodded. 'Anything else?'

'Most things that human beings do are a mystery.' She turned to Thora. 'Listen to Mr Walters. He knows the rules.'

At that moment Mr Walters appeared in their old canoe. He climbed out with an 'Oof'. Over his white pullover, he wore a bright orange life jacket. He removed a hanky from his pocket and dabbed his forehead. 'Hey, ho,' he said, tipping his bowler hat. 'I've moored the *Loki* in the harbour, but I'm afraid I haven't found us a place to stay as yet.'

Halla nodded and continued speaking to her daughter. 'I'll be here on the Rock. But don't come swimming back to me unless you really need to. I'll expect to see you for a short visit in three months' time.'

Thora was sad to be leaving, and for once she didn't mind her mother's nagging. They held hands and together looked over at the Grimli skyline.

'I wonder what causes that orange glow,' said Thora.

Halla shrugged. 'It's new,' she said. 'It wasn't there when you were a baby.'

Mr Walters jumped back into the canoe and pushed off with the end of his paddle. 'Cheerio,' he said to Halla. 'If you ever want to come out of retirement, you know where to find me.'

'My glory days are kaput,' said Halla. 'No more kick in the tail. And anyway, I need a rest. It will be heavenly just to sit and do nothing.'

'You'll always be Halla's Comet,' said Mr Walters, with feeling.

'You saved my life.' Halla blew kisses. Then to Thora she added, 'I'll be here if you need me.'

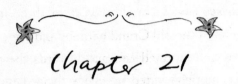

Chapter 21

The sea was choppy, the surface spread with restless peaks – like a birthday cake iced in a hurry.

Dusk was sifting down. Across the water, three or four kilometres away, the town threw off a sodium-orange glow.

'It's like somebody threw iodine at the sky,' observed Thora.

'An abomination,' agreed Mr Walters. 'Neon signs should be banned.'

Mr Walters did not love the idea of returning to Grimli, mainly on account of Frooty de Mare. He had not mentioned Frooty's letters to Thora and her mother, as he had not wanted to worry them. The lease belonged to him, fair and square. Even so, when Frooty heard about the return of the *Loki*, he was bound to pay them a visit. As always, the very thought of Frooty's name made Mr Walters think of wrecking balls.

With the Blue Bell Bed and Breakfast no longer in existence, they would have to walk through town to the cinema, where he would introduce Thora to the Greenberg sisters and ask them to recommend a nice place to stay.

He rather looked forward to seeing the three women again. *Especially* Flossie.

They entered the old Grimli harbour and glided past the bruised and battered *Loki* and towards the shore. Mr Walters was comforted by the fact that despite all the changes to the town, the harbour looked much as it had when they'd left it, ten years ago.

Thora broke the silence with a shout. 'Look up there!'

Sitting on an old oil drum at the end of the pier was a boy of about twelve. They passed so close beneath him that they could see the mosquito bites on his arms.

Thora waved. 'Ahoy!'

He was waiting with his dog and his bicycle on the jetty when they docked the boat. He wore a dirty yellow T-shirt and his ears stuck out.

'Hello. I'm Ricky. Welcome to Grimli. Population four thousand.'

'Four thousand plus three,' corrected Thora.

'Plans to stay?'

'Until I find my feet,' said Thora.

He looked down. 'Why? Have you lost them?'

'No,' she said. 'It's a figurine of speech.'

'Crikey!' he hollered. 'What's wrong with you? Your toes are *purple!*'

'Poor circulation. Runs in the family. Hey, are you like one of those boys in Tangiers who greet the Algeciras ferry and try to sell a night in their uncle's hotel?'

'Nope,' he said. 'I don't have an uncle and he don't have a hotel! But I could sell you a ride on my bike to the Tooty Frooty.'

'We're not staying there,' clipped Mr Walters.

'Really?' drawled Ricky. 'Everyone else does. Not much else going on here, except for the casino and the games room. Where have you come from?'

'The Rock,' answered Thora, leaping out of the canoe. She held out her hand for the dog to sniff.

'You're kidding!' Ricky whistled.

'Before that we were living between worlds. Ten years at sea and not one pirate ship!'

Ricky gave Thora a curious look. 'How did you do it? Get to the Rock, I mean. What was it like? And in a canoe!' He looked impressed. 'Tiny Stevens and me are gonna get there some day soon.'

His dog panted and wagged its stumpy tail.

Mr Walters frowned. 'No,' he said. 'It's a dreadful place. You don't want to go there. Teeming with leeches and jellyfish. Extremely dangerous. I'm surprised they haven't posted up warning signs.'

'Oh, they have,' said Ricky, 'but the winds take them down. There's a rip that runs alongside. The coast guard is always talking about it. We had to learn about it at school. And once a fisherman got lost near there. People round here stay clear of the Rock.' He looked out across the harbour. 'That's why I wanna go.'

'I would advise that you listen to the coast guard and to your teachers and stay away.' Mr Walters tipped his bowler hat at the boy and went off to have a word with the harbour master.

'There's nicer places to visit, anyway,' said Thora. She sat down on the pier to put on her windsurfing slippers. 'More constantinopalising places.'

Abruptly, a white truck pulled up at the pier and a very fat man jumped out. He was eating a hamburger and there were huge sweat stains under his armpits.

'Oh-oh,' said Ricky, spinning around. 'I gotta go.'

'Where have you been, you little brat? I told you to come right back home after you bought the lottery tickets,' the man shouted.

Ricky waved the tickets at Thora and sighed. Then he ran to the truck. 'I'm coming, *I'm coming.*'

The man pushed him roughly into the back of the truck. Then he stood there, finishing off his hamburger. When he had licked each of his ten fingers clean, he returned for the bicycle.

'Whaddina dog's breakfast are *you* looking at?' he spat at Thora.

'I'm not looking,' she replied primly. 'I'm staring.'

He lifted the bike up over his head and tossed it into the trailer. There was a crash as metal hit metal.

'Hey,' cried Thora. 'Don't forget your dog!'

The man jumped into the truck and drove off. The dog barked and ran after them.

'What was that all about?' asked Mr Walters, returning from the harbour master's office.

'Someone who got up on the wrong side of the Mid-Atlantic Ridge,' shrugged Thora.

Chapter 22

They headed off across the lengthening shadows of the dockyard, through a maze of peeling boathouses, spider webs and old rotting fish and rope smells.

Thora could hear the pitter-patter of mouse feet in the scaffoldings, the spongy clop of Mr Walters' Blundstone boots.

They emerged from the dockyard on to Grimli's main street just as the sun was dropping over the water. Mr Walters pointed. The Allbent Cinema was at the end of the next block.

Thora took a deep breath and hugged her bag close.

She was too excited to see Halla wave her goodnight from the Rock, now a dot on the pink water.

She took no notice of the people staring, or of Mr Walters, who hurried along ahead.

This was the street her father had walked.

This was the bakery where he had bought his cream doughnuts.

Here was the fish shop, the greengrocer, the butcher.

There was the cinema, where he'd had a job.

Some of these people might even have *spoken* to him.

Of course, she wasn't entirely sure about all of this, but she was quite sure that her father had liked cream doughnuts. Most people did!

Soon they came to a rather lopsided building with a crooked steeple and ornate windows. The Allbent Cinema.

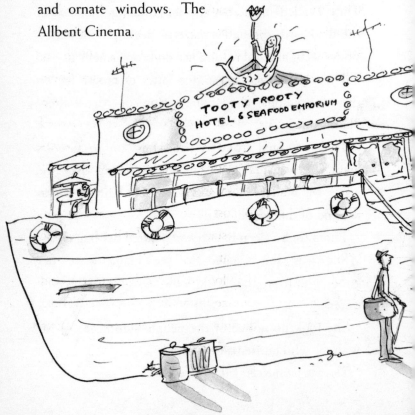

'It looks exactly like the Cistern Chapel in Rome,' enthused Thora, feeling a little homesick for her old life all of a sudden.

Mr Walters knocked and eventually a girl with mousy brown hair wearing a long black mohair jumper came to the door. She informed them that the sisters were away at the Venice Film Festival and would not be back for another month or so.

Mr Walters was crestfallen. 'Can you suggest a good bed and breakfast?'

'No, there aren't any. On the edge of town, a kilometre or so away, you'll find the Viking Motor Inn. Otherwise, the only place to stay is across the street.' She made a face. 'At the Tooty Frooty. It's a little grotty these days, but it depends whether you care about that sort of thing.'

Mr Walters and Thora crossed the street for a look. Mr Walters already knew what they would find.

It was one of those places that you almost always find in a seaside town. A restaurant–hotel built to resemble a boat.

It looked like a boat that would capsize instantly in the water, Thora thought as she examined its mauve and gold hull.

The sodium-orange sign read:

TOOTY FROOTY
HOTEL & SEAFOOD EMPORIUM.

Directly above the sign, a cartoon mermaid flicked her neon tail.

So *this* was what gave the town its mysterious glow.

'Tasteless,' remarked Mr Walters.

'Revulsive,' agreed Thora, heading up the steps. 'But that's not a good reason not to stay here while we repair the *Loki*.'

A large slit on the side of the hull blew a hot blast of onion-ring air right into Thora's face. Her ponytail stood straight up.

'A vile establishment,' said Mr Walters. 'As you shall see.'

He didn't try to stop Thora. He was accustomed to her investigations. He lit a cigar and found a shadow to stand in.

chapter 23

At the top of the steps, Thora pushed through the door. A large yellowing poster board greeted her.

At the end of a small, mirror-lined corridor, she passed into a crowded smoky room.

A party?

Nobody greeted her. Nobody even looked her way.

They all stood staring at the whirring, buzzing, glowing, pulsing, ringing television screens on the walls.

She tapped a man on the shoulder. 'Excuse me, sir. What are you doing?' she asked.

It was the grumpy man she'd seen at the pier with Ricky.

'Losing all my money,' he grunted. 'Shoo.'

'Shoo fly to you too,' said Thora indignantly.

She wandered up a little set of stairs and across a small wooden bridge. Down more stairs and into a large empty restaurant with floor-to-ceiling glass windows and a good view of the twinkling harbour. On one side was a marine display that included a stuffed mermaid. 'How odd,' said Thora. Lining the back wall was an enormous aquarium. GLUG GLUG GLUG. Where were the fish? The water was too murky to tell. The specials of the day were announced on a large sandwich board.

TODAY'S SPECIALS
MUDCAKE MASH

There was a desk. On the desk, a bell.

Thora rang the bell. It made a jangling noise.

'Hold your horses,' came a voice.

'I don't have any horses,' Thora shouted, 'only a peacock named Cosmo.'

A red-haired woman appeared. She wore a sort of sparkly tiara and a tight parrot-green top. A badge said MADGE. 'What can I do for you?' she asked.

'Any rooms for sale? A small room will do, preferably with a bunk bed each for me and my guardian and a bottom drawer for Cosmo here to sleep in.'

'Sorry, I'm not the person to speak to about rooms. You'll have to go back to the main entrance and turn left to get to the reception desk for the hotel. Look, save yourself the effort. There's an elevator over there.' She pointed.

'Does it work?'

'Should do.'

'Hah, then it's ripe to break down. I like my elevators out of service. Then you take the stairs and no worries, mate. We stayed once at one of the finest hotels in England. The Savoy Cabbage was the name. I got stuck in the elevator. Guess who was stuck with me?'

Madge shrugged. 'Old Liz?'

Thora guffawed. 'You mean Her Majesty? Are you kidding? The Queen doesn't take elevators.' Thora leaned forward. 'It was another kind of queen. The queen of the lawn-bowling circuit: Doris Danforth!'

Madge looked bored. 'Look, let me *show* you where the reception desk is.'

They passed close by the display of fake sea creatures and then headed up the stairs.

When they reached the reception desk Thora paused. 'What's that terrible racket?'

Madge held up her index finger. 'Shh.'

Behind the reception desk was a gold door marked *CEO, Tooty Frooty Enterprises*. The voice that stormed out from behind it was angry.

'After all I've done for this two-bit town – you'd

think you'd help me out on this one, you big meany!'

'Who's that?' asked Thora.

'The CEO of this dump,' said Madge through tight lips. 'Frooty de Mare.'

'Dump?' said Thora looking around. 'I don't see any rubbish.'

Madge snorted. 'Let me tell you, there's plenty of *that* around here.' She located the hotel register and opened it. 'Between you and me, Frooty's losing his marbles.'

Suddenly the door opened and Frooty stomped out, looking for his eyeglasses. When he had put them on, he glared at Thora.

'Who is this? What is going on?' he asked.

'I was just admiring the view,' said Thora pleasantly. 'But I must ask you ... why a stuffed mermaid when you could have a real one?'

'Listen, missy, if there was a real one to have, I'd have her,' he said. Then he stomped back into his office and slammed the door. Thora shivered.

'Between you and me, Madge, I gotta get going. Too many fake sea creatures here for my taste.'

Chapter 24

For one month, Mr Walters, Thora and Cosmo lived at the Viking Motor Inn on the edge of town. Mr Walters did not want Frooty de Mare sniffing around asking questions, and so he arranged for the *Loki* to be transported to a rented hangar near the airport. During the days, he and Thora worked very hard on repairs to the *Loki*. Ten years of round-the-world sailing had taken their toll. The hull was so encrusted with barnacles that it resembled a tortoise shell. The cabin bore the lashings of the wind and waves. Paint hung from the sides like the curling bark on a eucalyptus tree.

In the evenings, they read more books: Mr Walters, *Major General Sir John Hackett's World War III* and Thora, *The Complete Treasury of Falkland Islands Fables*.

They finished their repairs just as summer gave way to autumn and the air turned chilly.

Mr Walters peeled away the rug in the centre of the main room. It was a beautiful Turkish wool carpet with patterns of red and yellow diamonds and a gold fringe. It had been awarded to Halla after she swam the Bosphorus.

They had covered Halla's hole in the *Loki* with Plexiglas to keep out the chill of the sea. To open it, Thora simply had to slide back the glass. To take the edge off Thora's homesickness for the sea, they had also installed a 500-watt sea lamp from a swimming pool in Shreveport, Louisiana, which produced a cone of light that illuminated sea creatures in the sea below.

The hull sported a new coat of glossy white paint. The cabin had been enlarged. The roof re-tiled. When they transported the *Loki* back to the harbour, it looked like a brand new boat.

'All it needs now,' said Thora, 'are a few fenimen touches.'

'You mean feminine,' Mr Walters corrected.

'Sure,' said Thora.

Neither he nor Halla knew what living on land would do to Thora. He was pleased to see that so far she was prospering. Even if she wobbled over certain words.

To celebrate their return to the *Loki*, they had a party and broke a bottle of raspberry cordial over the stern. 'To the *Loki*!' they shouted merrily.

The mood was dampened by the arrival of a

telegram bearing sad news. That morning, Mr Walters'
dear brother, who was a sheep farmer, had died in Port
Desire, Argentina. His brother's son hoped very much
that Mr Walters might be able to attend the funeral.

He was not so sure that he wanted to leave Thora by
herself, but Thora insisted that she would be fine.

'The sisters will be back soon,' she said. 'I'll visit them
if I feel lonely.'

Mr Walters put a new chain belt around Thora's waist,
on to which he had welded five of Halla's medals.

'This is for good luck,' he said, and then from his suit

pocket he produced a fat cod-skin wallet stuffed with traveller's cheques.

'Make sure you get a good exchange rate.'

'Righty-o,' said Thora.

Mr Walters shook both her hands and kissed the top of her head. There was a sudden hiss. He jumped back. A jet of water sprayed out and drenched them both. Thora pulled her hair up and refastened her ponytail scrunchie. They both laughed. A mermaid's farewell never failed to take Mr Walters by surprise.

'Well, I'll be off,' he said. 'There will be some family business to settle after the funeral, but I'll be in touch. The time will pass faster than a shoal of fish.'

'Give it all you've got!' said Thora, giving him the thumbs-up signal. Her thumbs didn't seem to be working properly and her words sounded a little flat, so she added, 'Break a leg! Write if you remember!'

Mr Walters turned to Cosmo. 'Watch out for that beak of yours,' he said. 'No scratching the good wooden floors.' Then he turned back to Thora. 'He's good company,' he told her, 'even if he *is* a little vain.'

Thora watched Mr Walters climb into his taxi cab. 'Don't be sad, big fellow,' she said to Cosmo. 'Mr Walters will be back soon.' She did a cartwheel and landed with a *smuch!* in a small puddle of water.

Everything on the *Loki* was the same. And yet without Halla and now Mr Walters, it was completely different.

'Welcome home, Cosmo,' she said a little sadly.

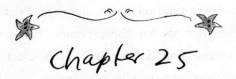

Chapter 25

The hardware store was dark and cramped and smelled of wood bits and gear-chains.

'What a cosy place,' Thora murmured, running her finger along the dusty shelves.

In the PAINT section she spun the colour wheel, settling for the colours that made her mouth water: three litres of Shrimp Pink, five litres of Quay-Lime Green.

In HOUSEWARES she selected an angel food cake tin, a set of blue tin cups and an oven mitt in the shape of a flounder.

The woman behind the counter reached for Thora's basket. 'Will that be all?'

Thora scratched her chin thoughtfully. 'I'm doing a little *inner decorating*,' she said. 'Could you add a few walls of that wallpaper to my bill, please? The furry green variety?'

'That's not wallpaper,' said the woman. 'It's indoor–outdoor carpet.'

'Fine,' said Thora coolly. 'I'll take ten square metres.'

She was not entirely sure what a square metre was, but luckily the woman seemed to know.

'Oh, and one last thing! I'd like a dozen pink flamingos. The plastic ones, of course. Real flamingos are impractical birds for these climes, but a dozen plastic flamingos will do the trick. Now what is the rate of exchange for a traveller's cheque?'

'Gosh, I haven't seen one of those in years!'

'Same as cash!' said Thora.

After she left the store she returned to the pier and set up the pink flamingos in a line on the deck of the *Loki*.

She rolled out the carpet and hung it on her bedroom wall.

Then with the pink and quay-lime paint she made up a sign and nailed it on to the cabin door:

TRESSPASSERS WILL BE PROSTLETYSED.

She was having so much fun that she made another sign:

MAID, PLEASE MAKE UP MY ROOM.

And another:

NO LOITERING, SPITTING,
OR RUNNING ON DECK.

'A girl can't run on empty,' she said to Cosmo. She reached for a large glass bowl and whipped up a batter of egg whites, sugar, cream of tartar and flour and poured it into her new angel food cake tin. Soon the old smell of Mr Walters' cigar smoke and Irish Spring aftershave was mingling with the sweet smell of baking cake. She sat herself down and sipped a cup of Russian Caravan tea with a good dash of warm milk and three lumps of brown sugar. Finally, she pulled an old fedora of Mr Walters' over her eyes and stretched out on the floor to catch a few winks.

'When the paint dries, we'll have to give some very serious consideration to the furniture and inner decorations. Really, Cosmo, we have *barely scratched the surface!*'

Chapter 26

Thora was awoken very early the next morning by a tremendous vibrating noise in the sky.

'Jeepers!' she cried, leaping out of bed. 'What's all this kakka-phony? Oh look, Cosmo! It's an arrow-plane!'

Cosmo burrowed his head into the breadbox and whimpered.

Thora opened the door and rushed out on to the pier. She had seen a number of aircraft in her time, but never one with flashing gold wings.

For a moment she wondered if it wasn't some overgrown parrot on its way to the Amazon. But then the wings dipped, and as the plane turned she could see the cockpit and a number of white faces pressed against the glass.

Trailing after it, like a long ribbon, was a banner.

FROOTY DE MARE'S CELEBRATION CONTINUES: SAMPLE OUR WORLD-FAMOUS SHRIMP PIE & ONION RINGS!

The plane did a somersault and headed back the way it had come.

There is something about an aeroplane that makes one look up and wave. With the exception of a fisherman hauling his nets into his boat, Thora was quite alone on the pier that morning. She waved at the swooping plane. Somebody in the cockpit waved back.

'I say, mister,' she shouted to the fisherman, 'isn't it a wonderful show!'

The old fisherman shook his head and removed his earplugs. Thora repeated herself. The fisherman flicked his hand. 'Nah, it's a bleeding nuisance. He does it every Saturday morning. That's why I wear these.'

'Cosmo is like you,' said Thora. 'But I *love* the noise. It reminds me of the helicopters in Marrakech! They were always buzzing around us when my mother went to open their Roman swimming pool. Very exhilarating!'

The fisherman made a face. 'Don't be fooled,' he said, and disappeared into the cabin of his boat.

The plane performed a few more tricks before landing in the harbour. Out of nowhere, an official-looking boat with quivering antennae sprinted across the water and stopped beside the plane. The door of the plane opened. A ladder dropped down. Led by a bad-tempered man in a black leather coat, six people climbed out.

The coast guard delivered them to the pier. The man stepped on to it and yelled at his sons to help their mother with her bags. 'I have people to meet. Places to go. Get a move-on!'

Thora would have known that voice anywhere. It sounded like rust and grit and wet sand.

She had heard it at the Tooty Frooty.

It was the man with the silly name: Frooty de Mare.

He rushed off, leaving three hulking sons with shaved heads and baggy jeans, a short, round, fusspot woman in a yellow scarf, and finally, lagging behind the group, with a faraway look in her eyes, a much younger girl. She had wonderful dark curly hair and wore an old-fashioned red tartan kilt and shiny patent-leather shoes. She was no more than ten metres from Thora.

'Hey, cur!' yelled Thora. 'Over here!'

Chapter 27

Holly was about to follow her mother on to the de Mares' very large family cabin cruiser when Thora stuck out her tongue.

It was the longest tongue Holly had ever seen. And above the tongue were the greenest green eyes Holly had ever seen.

She was alarmed by the CLANG of the medals around the girl's waist and by the ponytail that sprouted from the top of her head and by the weird black rubber suit she wore.

Suddenly the tongue snapped back into the girl's mouth and she rubbed her tummy. 'Yum,' she said. 'It's rude to gape. Didn't your mother teach you that? Mine did, before she swam out between the icebergs in Hudson's Bay. I was gaping at a polar bear at the time.'

Holly's bow lips formed a perfect 'O'.

'Excellent way to trap a fly,' said Thora.

Holly quickly covered her mouth.

'You see,' continued Thora, 'when the polar bear saw me staring, he charged at me and would have eaten me if I hadn't dropped to the ground and pretended to be dead. Polar bears, *Ursus maritimus*, are flesh-eating mammals. They prefer girls with long black curly hair and tartan kilts. But there are so few of them up north that they have to settle for skinny girls with brown hair and itchy elbows.' She scratched her elbows, first one and then the other.

Holly looked around. 'There aren't any polar bears in Grimli.' She paused. 'Are there?'

'I believe not,' Thora assured her. 'Sadly. And anyway, polar bears prefer tough meat to tender. So you are automatically disqualified.'

Holly stiffened.

To cheer her up, Thora began a dance, a little Highland fling that Mr Walters had taught her. 'Of course, it isn't the same without bagpipes. If I could borrow your bladder for a second we could straighten that out.'

'My *bladder*?'

'Bagpipes are made out of bladders. Mr Walters is one-quarter Scottish. He told me all about it. The old Scotsmen were very good inventors. Take your kilt, for instance. They invented tartan. They liked it so much that the men wore tartan skirts to fight in wars! Imagine! Brave soldiers in skirts! What a funny place.'

'Who's Mr Walters?'

'My human Guardian Angle.'

Holly looked puzzled.

'Anyway,' continued Thora, 'in Scotland my mother swam Loch Ness. She had to drop out because of the Loch Ness monster. But they were on very good terms by the time we left. We even had Nessie aboard for scones and a drop of warming Scotch whisky.'

Holly frowned.

'Oh dear,' said Thora, 'I've upset you again. Maybe we can start again over a nice cup of Russian Caravan tea.' She jumped from the pier on to the *Loki*. 'Come on in. The air is fine!'

'I don't drink tea,' said Holly, following her on to the deck and into the cabin. 'It contains tannic acid and other harmful additives.'

'Then how about some octopus cheeks? I believe we have a few leftovers. I can reheat them in a jiffy.' She began to light the gas stove with a long wooden match.

'I'm not allowed to play with matches.'

'Play? We're not *playing*,' Thora laughed.

'That's my mother calling me,' said Holly suddenly. 'I have to go, right now!'

'No worries,' said Thora brightly. 'There's a luxury toilet that-a-way! It even has an electric velvet seat cover to warm your bottom.'

Holly blushed. 'That's not at all what I meant,' she

said, reaching for the door. 'My mother will be wondering where I am. Goodbye …'

'Drop by for tea any time!' shouted Thora. 'We were only just getting warmed up!'

Chapter 28

Frooty rushed down the pier towards his office in the Tooty Frooty. He did not even notice that the *Loki* now occupied the berth he had once been so desperate to get hold of. His mind was too full of his latest great idea.

It had come to him in the dead of night. That was how it usually worked with geniuses. He'd been thinking his usual thoughts about how to get rid of the Greenberg sisters. How he hated those old hags! He'd had his sons unleash rats in the aisles of the Allbent and tried to have it declared a public health hazard. He'd tried to burn them down, freeze them up, smoke them out. But so far, nothing had worked. People kept going to their dingy old cinema to see their boring arty-farty movies. He just didn't get it.

Anyway, as he tossed and turned in the bed that he shared with Mrs de Mare, the idea came to him.

If you can't get rid of them, beat them at their own game!

He'd open up his own cinema and pinch their customers!

Once the idea took hold, it had taken him only six weeks to build a triplex cinema seating 300 people, on a lot once occupied by a waterfront bed and breakfast. When it opened in one month's time, he would throw a big party and invite the whole town – except for the Greenberg sisters, of course. Plans were well underway for a Dixieland band and an all-you-can-eat smorgasbord.

He just needed a name.

Chapter 29

A week or so after Holly's visit, Thora was mending cobwebs on the ceiling of her little cabin when it began to rain.

Cold, fat drops from a stone-coloured sky.

Something about the quality of the light reminded Thora of November in Venice.

Venice made her think of the Allbent Cinema.

'It's time to see if the sisters are back,' she said to herself.

She tied a plastic flowered rain bonnet on to Cosmo's head and they headed off to the cinema.

To Thora's surprise, the streets were deserted.

'In India, they would be out celebrating the rain!' She performed a little dance she had been taught in Calcutta during a monsoon. 'Maybe the residents of Grimli just don't appreciate water the way we do.'

A sign in the window of Gulli's Goodies took Thora by surprise.

'How unfortunate,' she said. 'Cupcakes taste best in the rain.'

The Tooty Frooty gave off a lonely air. Even the builders on Frooty's latest construction site were silent.

Thora began to whistle a song she had learned from the Xanti in the Amazon. It was a very sad tune in a minor key about a girl who had lost her lover and was weeping by the river where he'd been eaten by an anaconda.

The sad tune and the pelting rain all round her made her long for Halla. The pumpkin smell of her hair. Her bedtime kisses.

She hoped that her mother was safe from anacondas.

She stood for a minute staring at the water she could see in the gap between the buildings. The colour of the sea was always changing. It was always worth a look. Today it was grey, grey, grey.

Except for a bright bit of red flashing between the waves.

Thora had excellent vision. But she could hardly believe her eyes when she saw that the flashing red bit in the water was in fact her very own canoe!

What was it doing out at sea? Surely Mr Walters hadn't returned to Grimli without telling her!

She stared hard.

The person in the boat was moving around so much it was hard to focus. When she did, she saw thin arms covered with red mosquito bites. 'Ricky!' she said to Cosmo. 'The boy from the pier!'

A gust of wind caught her ponytail. She turned around and saw a police car speed by. Then came the sound of an ambulance and several people shouting and running towards the beach. He must be in danger!

Chapter 30

By the time Thora got to the beach, a crowd had formed. A few people glanced her way but nobody spoke to her. They were all staring and pointing out to sea at the boy in the red canoe. Everyone was talking at once.

'He stole the boat from the dockyards.'

'He's *always* running away.'

'He's caught in a rip.'

'Why is the coast guard taking so long?'

'I don't think he's even wearing a life jacket.'

Then a pale woman fell to her knees and began to sob. 'He doesn't know how to swim! Somebody, please save him!'

Thora reckoned that this must be Ricky's mother.

'Come on, Cosmo,' she whispered. 'We don't have a lot of time.'

Thora headed down the beach. When she was out of sight of the crowd, she slipped into the heaving water. Up close it looked less grey and more green, the colour of the sage leaves that Mr Walters liked to sprinkle on his rice pudding. She dived down deep and began to swim.

The strength of the rip surprised her. She was breathing hard when she surfaced, remembering the massive rips in the sea at Bilgola Beach in Sydney. Halla had taught her how to swim diagonally against the pulling water. She did this now as she approached the canoe from the ocean side, careful to keep her head low so that the people on shore couldn't see her.

She steered the canoe at an angle and turned it so that it faced the shore.

Ricky stopped paddling and looked over his shoulder. The wind had messed up his hair, his cheeks were red and he had a wild look in his dark eyes. 'What are *you* doing here?' he shouted above the wind.

Thora steadied the boat and continued pushing.

'You're caught in the rip,' she said.

'No,' said Ricky. 'Let me go.'

'If I let you go, you'll be swept out to sea.'

'Let go!' he shouted. 'I don't want to go home!'

'Right-o,' said Thora, letting go.

The canoe spun around like a bottle and shot off. Ricky lost his balance and almost toppled overboard. 'Help!'

She swam after him. 'You changed your mind yet?'

'Yes!' he cried. Immediately, he looked as if he regretted it.

'I'll help you on one condition.'

'What?'

'Don't mention me.'

'Why?'

'I'm undercover.'

'You're *what?*' The sea was pulling him away fast. 'All right, all right,' he shouted. 'Whatever you say.'

Thora righted the boat and guided it out of the rip. The muscular tug of the water against them was using up her strength. She wished Halla were there to help.

Like an echo of her thoughts, there was a *click*.

The wind died. A soft *whoosh*.

Thora felt a soft, warm breeze at her back. The boat glided along, effortlessly. Thora removed her fingertips. It continued towards shore as if propelled by its own invisible engine.

'Thanks, Mother,' whispered Thora to the waves.

Chapter 31

Before they opened the Allbent Cinema, Lottie, Flossie and Dottie Greenberg were three glamorous sisters with an interest in clothes and movie stars. Here is a photo of them when they were young.

Lottie was the brain. Flossie the feisty one. Dottie the dreamer. They were stylish and vivacious, and worked in part-time jobs in town. Flossie in the bakery where she iced cupcakes and decorated the gingerbread men in cricket whites and trilby hats; Lottie as a teller at the bank; Dottie as a seamstress and dressmaker.

Twice a year they took the cross-channel ferry to Boulogne and returned wearing the latest Continental fashions: silk scarves, oversized sunglasses, animal-patterned handbags, odd little boots lined with poodle fur. There clung to them an air of otherworldliness that both repelled and fascinated, like strong perfume. It might not be to your taste, but you got used to it after a while.

The sisters thought nothing of changing their hair colour, piercing their ears, or sunbathing on the pier in two-piece bathing suits. Not uncommon today, but it was considered racy back then. They took long walks together, flew kites in the park, kept a pet lizard on the radiator in their sun room and even roller-skated to work when they felt like it.

They had boyfriends, although never anything very serious. They always intended to get married but somehow never got around to it. Sisters can be lazy about certain things when they have each other to fall back on.

They liked their life just the way it was.

It was during a trip to Venice that the sisters fell in love for the first time – with the movies. But Grimli had no cinema! When the old Anglican church was struck by lightning, and the minister moved his congregation across town, the sisters pooled their cash and bought the building. They named it the Allbent because the lightning had hit the church steeple and the building leaned a little to the left.

A film screen from Hollywood, California, was installed. A projector was purchased from a travelling spiritualist in a caravan. Seats were bought at auction.

On the cinema's opening night, every seat was full, and within a month the Allbent was the most popular place in town.

If you listened, you could hear the mysterious sounds of the cinema from any point in town.

On Mondays, the sound of people swooning. On Tuesdays, laughter. Wednesdays, weeping. Thursdays, cries of fright and horror. Fridays, sighs. And on the weekends a little bit of everything. It was as if the projector were capable of giving life and colour to every emotion experienced by the inhabitants of the small seaside town.

And so Dottie's announcement that she was going to have a baby was received by her sisters with surprising calm. The theatre seemed to make everybody feel more alive, more optimistic. It was altogether a very happy environment for a baby to be born and grow up in.

✳

On this rainy day, when everything in town was either flooded or closed, a welcoming light shone through the steamed-up stained-glass windows of the Allbent.

Thora opened the door and took a deep breath of the buttery-smelling lobby air. The three great windows, composed of blue, yellow and red glass, lent the lobby a celestial aura.

On the walls were posters of famous old movie stars. Greta Garbo, Clark Gable, Vivien Leigh. There were also posters of more recent movie stars, but in colour they were not nearly so glamorous.

The girl behind the counter in the black mohair jumper was painting her nails purple. 'Movie starts in three minutes,' she said without looking up.

'I came to meet the Greenberg sisters. I would have come sooner, but I've been busier than an octopus on a construction site.'

'The Greenbergs are still away,' said the girl, who wore a name badge that read KAT.

Thora absorbed the news with a frown. 'When will they be back?'

'End of the month. It's their annual trip to Venice to see the new movies.'

Suddenly Thora felt quite lonely. She wished she had some friends. She wished that Halla was waiting at the *Loki*, ready to greet her with a nice cup of Russian Caravan Tea.

When Kat saw her lip tremble, she held out a box of tissues. 'Twenty pence each,' she said. 'You'll have the theatre to yourself today. The rain has kept everyone away. Nobody will see you crying.'

'I seem to cry at the flick of a tail these days,' said Thora, helping herself. 'Maybe it's all the rain we're getting. And then there's Cosmo. He looks so glum most of the time that he makes *me* want to cry. Together we really are a field and valley of tears.' She paid and went in.

In some ways, it was just an ordinary old-fashioned theatre, with rows of dusty plush velvet seats and heavy maroon curtains and steep aisles that felt sticky underfoot.

But Thora, who had never been inside a cinema before, looked around her in wonder. The chandelier overhead reminded her of a great jewelled fish. The organ at the front resembled the pipe organ she'd glimpsed in a Greek Orthodox church in Thessalonika. She found a sèat in the front row. As the lights dimmed and the screen filled with coloured images, she felt right at home.

It was just like swimming underwater.

For two full hours, Thora forgot about everything

except the story unfolding before her. The movie featured a family torn apart by war. There was a beautiful daughter with a slim waist, a lover with a moustache and many rousing battle scenes. When the movie finished, she stood up and stretched and flopped back into her squeaky chair, hoping to make the feeling last. Eventually, Kat shone her flashlight in Thora's face and asked her to leave.

'I could watch that again and again and again,' sighed Thora.

'I do,' said Kat. 'Sometimes three times per day.'

'You are so lucky to work in a cinema. They're very romantic places, aren't they? The movie was a bit sad, but that's what I liked about it. Quite different from the sadness that real life throws one's way.' She punched her chest. 'That,' she added, 'is the opposite of delicious.'

She clasped Kat's hand. 'Maybe *I* might get a job here. What do you think? You wouldn't even have to pay me. I could sweep up sweets wrappers and popcorn kernels – that sort of thing.'

'We don't need any help,' said Kat coldly.

'But we *all* need a little help,' said Thora. 'My mother always says, "Don't kick a gift sea horse in the mouth." I'm Thora, by the way.'

Kat followed Thora to the door.

'I'll be back,' said Thora. 'Goodbye.'

'Not so fast,' said Kat. 'What is *this*?' She shone the

torch on Thora's feet. She then followed the wet trail back into the cinema, to Thora's seat. 'I don't believe it! You've spilled your drink everywhere!'

'Must be from the rain,' sang Thora. 'I didn't have a drink.'

'I'll bet you don't do this at home.'

'Well, now that you mention it . . .'

'Did you wet your pants?'

'Course not,' said Thora, laughing. What a silly thing to say.'

'You're calling me silly?'

'I suppose I am.'

'*Just go*,' said Kat, pushing the mop across the floor.

After Kat had put the mop away and locked the front doors and turned off the television set and the popcorn machine, she took out a new piece of white chalk.

Under the word BANISHED she added another name.

Thora.

Chapter 32

Meanwhile, word had got around Grimli that a strange girl was living alone on the *Loki* with her pet peacock. At the regular Monday town council meeting, parents and teachers stood up and declared that no child should be living without adult supervision. On Tuesday, the Children's Aid Society was contacted. Foster parents were alerted. On Wednesday, a photograph of Thora appeared in the *Daily Seasider*, along with an urgent appeal.

Abandoned child needs home!

Thora is approximately ten years old. She is energetic and resourceful and at present does not seem to realise that she has been abandoned by a certain Mr Walters. She appears to love animals and bright colours and possibly onion rings. If you can be a foster parent to this little girl,

please contact Mrs Honey Grubb via the Grimli
Police Station.

Thora howled as she read the evening paper. 'Listen
to this, Cosmo. They say I am *little*! Imagine!' She stood
up to remind Cosmo that she was tall for her age.
Cosmo nodded. 'I suppose I do love bright colours.
And animals. But certainly not Doberman pinschers or
March flies or scorpions. And terns are a bit scary.
Remember when we were in Bass Strait and that tern
dive-bombed Mr Walters and pecked his scalp?' She
shivered and gave Cosmo a hug. 'But *you're* all right.
Now, off to the bakery to get something to eat!'

Thora and Cosmo were sprawled on the floor stuffing themselves with cream doughnuts when they heard the clop-clop-clopping of hooves on the dock.

Thora raced to the window. 'Here's a sight for sore eyes!' she shouted. Cosmo coughed and scratched. 'Do you think he's for real?' Thora asked.

The policeman climbing down off his horse was a magnificent sight, in his tight scarlet tunic with its shiny gold buttons and his breeches and his knee-high leather boots. He whistled as he made his way over to the *Loki*.

'I'm looking for a girl named Thora,' he said through the door.

Thora swallowed and nodded and threw open the door and pointed at herself. 'Well, you found her,' she said.

'I've been asked to pay you a little visit.'

'Lucky me,' enthused Thora. 'A real, live grenadier. *Do* come in.' She ushered the big man into the *Loki* and offered him a seat on an old apple crate and then handed him a doughnut. 'I haven't laid eyes on one of you since a member of your troupe arrested my mother in Buenos Aires for taking a dip in a fish tank.'

'Sorry to disappoint you,' he said, 'but I'm a police officer.'

'No need to be sorry!' she said. 'I'm not!'

It was then that she noticed that Cosmo had eaten the cream out of all the doughnuts. She was wondering what to do, as it seemed a bit mean to serve doughnuts without cream, when the crate the policeman was sitting on collapsed underneath him.

'Oops-a-daisy!' he said, springing to his feet.

Thora scooped up his doughnut and rushed into the bathroom. She searched for Mr Walters' shaving kit. 'Phew!' she said, flipping the cap off a tall green bottle marked BRUTE SHAVING CREAM – FOR ALL SKIN TYPES. She shook it and pressed the top, and hey presto, a wonderful dollop of soft white foam appeared. She was so pleased that she shook and squirted a few more times.

Then she ran back and handed the officer the doughnut.

He admired it and took a bite.

'Fresh from the bakery an hour ago,' she said. She had never sampled shaving cream before. The smell was a little musky for her taste. 'How is it?' she asked, anxiously.

'Delicious!'

'There's more!' she cried, delighted. 'Won't be a minute.'

In the bathroom she squirted what was left of the shaving cream on to the remaining doughnuts. 'Excuse my fingers,' she said, handing one to the policeman.

'Never mind,' he said, with his mouth full of doughnut. 'Now, getting back to the reason I came. It seems that you are living here all by yourself. Correct?'

'Incorrect.'

The policeman checked the notes on his clipboard. 'Hmm,' he said. 'Do you mind if I sit over there?' He pointed to the big leather chair. He looked a little unwell.

'Please do,' said Thora.

'Now,' resumed the policeman. 'It says here that you are an orphan. I'm to help you gather your things together and then you are to come with me to headquarters, where we'll meet Mrs Grubb, who will take you to meet the Rukles, your new foster family.'

'Frosted family?' said Thora, laughing. 'Now I've heard everything!' She sprang across the room and grabbed the policeman's hand. 'I know a good game! It's called Statues!' She pulled him to his feet and spun him around.

'Now, now,' he said. 'Be a good girl and do as I say.'

'No, you be a good policeman and do as *I* say. When I let go of your hand, you have to stand the way you land – frozen to the ground – and you're not allowed to move a muscle. That's why it's called Statues. Then when I press a button on your jacket, you come to life. If you're a *good* statue, and by that I mean an *interesting* statue, the rich art expert might decide to purchase you for a museum. I play the art expert. OK? Ready? Here we go!'

'I don't feel at all well,' said the policeman, falling on all fours.

'Ssshh!' Thora let her ponytail fall into her face. She scratched her elbows. She snapped her fingers. 'Got it. You're a husky dog named … King, pulling an Inuit across the tundra. Mush! Mush!'

The policeman stood up. His tunic was streaked with shaving cream and his breeches were dusty from the floor. He headed for the door in fright.

'That's the broom cupboard!'

Too late. The broom and mop bumped him on the head.

'Don't you hate it when that happens!' sang Thora.

The policeman groaned.

'Let's get you some fresh air,' said Thora. She guided him outside and with an encouraging pat on the back, she helped him mount his horse. 'Come back any time.

But be sure to call first. Then I can make sure that there are lots of cream doughnuts for you when you get here!'

'Oh, please, no!' he cried, and galloped off as fast as the horse's legs would carry him.

'Husky dogs don't talk!' she cried out after him.

Cosmo squawked.

'Yikes!' said Thora. 'Some people don't understand the first thing about playing Statues!'

chapter 33

'*Food poisoning?!*' shrieked Mrs Grubb, the mayor's wife.

'Food poisoning,' said the Chief of Police.

'But he was sent there to collect the orphan, not to have a dinner party!'

'All I can tell you, Mrs Grubb, is that he came back from the *Loki* green as a tree frog. Threw up all over the front steps of the police station. Looked like cream doughnuts to me. I sent him home with orders to stay in bed until it passes.'

'How you people can call yourselves professionals . . .'

'Sorry, ma'am. Want *me* to go and net her?'

'No. I'll do it myself.'

That evening, the Chief of Police delivered Thora a handwritten invitation from the mayor's wife:

Dear Thora,

I would be very charmed to meet you.
Would you like to come for lunch tomorrow?
We shall eat egg salad sandwiches, tapioca pudding and a beverage of your choice. We can discuss your future here in Grimli and how I can help you.
Please drop in to 12 Vegemewler Street at noon.

Yours sincerely,
Mrs Honey Grubb.

'Tickety-boo, Cosmo!' cried Thora. 'Our first lunch party on dry land!'

Thora remembered her mother's words about taking a present when paying someone a visit. That night, she stayed up very late baking an octopus-cheek casserole. From the pewter tea chest she pulled out a small figurine of Neptune that her mother had found on the bed of the great Icelandic salmon river, Langa. It was black and made of lava and thought to have been carved by one of the early Irish monks who sailed to Iceland in a coracle in the fifth century. She put it in a small box, sprinkled some of Cosmo's neck fluff on it in case it got knocked about, and put it in the pocket of her Halla-Skin.

At noon the next day, Thora rang the bell of 12 Vegemewler Street. Mrs Honey Grubb greeted her wearing a yellow trousersuit, rubber gloves and a surgical mask. In one hand she carried a bottle of room spray. Her honey-coloured hair was pulled back severely. She had small black eyes in a large flat face. She welcomed Thora in with a *Pssssss! Pssssss!* from her spray bottle.

'Did I interrupt something?' coughed Thora.

She bowed and held out her hand, but Mrs Grubb did not take it. Instead, Mrs Grubb removed her mask and let it dangle around her neck like a necklace.

'I was just doing a spot of dusting,' she explained. 'Do come in. How lovely to see you, Thora. And look! Don't tell me you've brought some food! You shouldn't have, really. You're going to show me up!'

Thora handed Mrs Grubb the casserole and glanced around the living room. The furniture, including a piano, was covered with what looked like cling-film. The plants were fake, the carpet was streaked with vacuum stripes and the lights were of a fluorescence so bright that it hurt Thora's eyes. The room reminded Thora of the quarantine station in London where they'd been forced to board Cosmo back when Halla swam the English Channel.

'Do excuse my gloves,' said Mrs Grubb, sniffing the

casserole. 'I have a *condition*. I wear them to protect my immune system.'

'Oh yes,' enthused Thora. 'I totally agree.'

'With what?'

'It is *very important* to protect both the solar system *and* the moon system. I think the moon system must feel a little left out sometimes, what with the sun getting all the attention. Personally, I prefer the moon. It's prettier, and you can look at it without hurting your eyes.'

Mrs Grubb frowned. 'My immune system was depleted last year because of all the charity work I do. My husband, the mayor, is always at me to slow down and put myself first. You see, I'm one of those people who sees a problem and just *has to help*. Some people are born that way, you know. The problem is, I've worn out my immune system and now I am allergic to hairspray, nail polish remover, perfume, tomatoes, water, air and *especially* to peacocks. I'm afraid you cannot bring that beast with you. You're going to have to get rid of it eventually. It's against the rules for foster children to bring their pets to their new house. But for now, tie it to the fence post. Here's a chain. I always keep several on hand. You never know when you might need one.'

'Oh, that's not necessary,' said Thora. 'Cosmo will head on home by himself.'

Thora waved Cosmo goodbye and followed Mrs Grubb into the dining room. The air was stuffy and the room smelled like a sanitised public loo. Thora's eyes and nose began to water.

'I knew it,' said Mrs Grubb. 'A sickly orphan girl.'

'Where?' asked Thora, looking around.

Mrs Grubb handed her a box of tissues. 'Have a blow,' she said. 'I always keep them on hand just in case.'

'Oh, that's OK. I usually just use my sleeve.'

'Poor thing. You haven't been *socialised*, have you?'

'Well, I'm not sure, what's that?'

'Nobody has taken the time to teach you *manners*. To teach you how a young lady ought to behave.' She opened a closet door and pulled out a bag. 'But all that is about to change.' Her lips tightened. 'Here's a little something to get you launched into your new life.'

'A present? For me? That's very thoughtful!' said Thora, touching the box in her pocket containing the statue of Neptune. Somehow, she didn't think Mrs Grubb would like it. Mrs Grubb passed her the bag and she removed the bundle that was inside. It was wrapped in yellow tissue paper. Thora sneezed. 'What is it?'

'A dress,' said Mrs Grubb.

'Thank you, but I don't really wear dresses,' said Thora, recalling her mother's warning about hiding her scales.

'It's not just *any* dress,' said Mrs Grubb sharply. 'It's a school uniform!'

'You're kidding!' laughed Thora, holding it up. 'But I don't go to school.'

'You will soon. Now, try it on. There's a bathroom over there. Don't dawdle!'

In the bathroom, Thora pulled the dress on over her wetsuit. It was made from a light cotton material with a pattern of blue and white checks. It had a Peter Pan collar and buttons up the front.

'It's not very waterproof,' said Thora, as she emerged from the bathroom.

'Silly girl! First you'll have to remove that dreadful black suit you're wearing.'

'My Halla-Skin? That's impossible!' said Thora.

'Don't be ridiculous. Take it off this instant, and then I'll take you over to the school and enrol you, and then we'll go and meet your foster family, the Rukles.'

'No,' said Thora slowly. 'You see, I have a "condition" myself.'

Mrs Grubb narrowed her eyes. 'Is that right?'

'Yes, ma'am.'

'Well, I can't say I'm surprised. All that sneezing! That running nose! What is it?'

'It's called *Diam Rem*.'

'I don't think I've heard of that one. *Diam Rem*. Hmm. Is that the Latin name? Let me get my *Big Book of Common Illnesses and Ailments*.'

'No!' cried Thora. 'It won't be in there ... it's not very *common*.'

'A rare condition. Is it contagious?'

'Only if I remove my Halla-Skin.'

Mrs Grubb frowned. 'Is it fatal?'

'Not exactly. It's more of a ... *choronic* sort of condition. I'll have it for the rest of my life. It's something I've had to learn to live with. I'm used to it now, but I need to spend a lot of time near water. Outside, you know. That's why school won't work out very well.'

'All children must attend school. Especially orphans in need of socialisation. Anyway, I've never heard of it.' She sniffed. '*Diam Rem*. Were you diagnosed by a proper doctor or a quack?'

Thora leaned forward and pulled up one of the legs of her wetsuit to reveal a purple ankle. Under the fluorescent light, her scales came into sharp focus.

Mrs Grubb gasped and reached for her face mask. 'Let us be off!'

Chapter 34

First, Mrs Grubb took Thora to the local primary school. Although the term did not begin for another month, she wanted Thora to meet the headteacher. 'There's someone I want to introduce you to,' she told her.

The school was a long, low building the colour of pale sand, and on the main door, a sign read:

You are now entering a QUIET ZONE.
Visitors report to Main Office.

'Oh dear,' said Thora. 'We didn't bring flowers!'

'Flowers?'

Thora pointed to the sign. 'When Mr Walters had his hip replacement operation I used to visit him at the hostable in Salisbury, and these signs were everywhere.'

'This is not a hospital. It's a school.'

'A school?' said Thora. 'But I thought schools were

made out of red brick and had a bell at the entrance and a fire escape out the side. At least, that's what the school looks like in *Tom Brown's School Days.'*

They made their way down a long empty corridor with gleaming linoleum floors that creaked underfoot. 'It certainly smells like a hostable. Well, actually, it smells a little like your house, Mrs Grubb.'

'That's the disinfectant,' said Mrs Grubb. 'Not something I'd expect that you've come across very often in your life.'

In a small office stacked with papers, books and brown cardboard boxes, Mrs Grubb folded away her face mask and pressed a buzzer. 'He said he'd meet us in here. Now, where is he?'

You are now entering a QUIET ZONE
visitors report to Main office

Thora ran over to the other side of the room and picked a book up off a trolley. '*Harry Potter and the Philosopher's Stone*. I wonder if this book is about Mr Walters' artist friend, the hairy potter from Cape Town.'

'I doubt it,' said Mrs Grubb.

'He had the bushiest, blackest moustache I've ever seen. And a beard, and a ponytail down to his waist which he fastened with a twist-tie! He even had tufts of hair sprouting out of his ears and from the tops of his fingers! Oh, and before I forget, he also had hair on his chest and his back. He said it was terribly hot in the summer, like wearing a black sheepskin vest around, and that he'd thought about having it all removed, zapped with a laser, like an Olympic swimmer does.'

'My goodness, you do rabbit on.'

'Interestingly, he didn't have any hair on the top of his head. His hairline started just above his ears.' She fluffed out her ponytail. 'Mr Walters said that hair patterns are inherited through the mother's line. So the potter must have had a very interesting-looking mother!'

'I can't abide hairy men. He sounds horrid.'

'Oh no, he was a sparky person and very good at his trade. He let me have a go on his potter's wheel, but I'm afraid my pot caved in. Potting requires a delicate touch. Have you ever thrown a pot, Mrs Grubb?'

'I may take it up if you don't shut up. You're making my sinuses ache. Oh, now, here he comes. Hello, Mr Mason!'

'I'm sorry to keep you waiting.'

'Think nothing of it. We were just admiring all your excellent books, weren't we, Thora?'

'I'd love to read this book about Mr Walters' friend, the hairy potter from Cape Town.'

Mr Mason gave a puzzled smile. 'A fine book! And a favourite with many children. It's great to see them reading. As a headteacher you can't ask for much more, can you? Heh heh heh. You may borrow it if you like.'

'Thanks,' sang Thora, tucking it into the pocket in her wetsuit, next to the little statue of Neptune.

'Now,' said Mrs Grubb, 'we were hoping to register Thora so she can start school next term.'

Mr Mason pulled out a pile of papers from a drawer in his desk. 'OK, let's get the ball in motion here. Let me see. What year are you in at the moment, Thora?'

'I'm afraid I don't understand the question.'

'How far have you progressed with your formal education?'

'I've never gone to school. So I reckon not very far, formally.'

'Never?'

'Nope.'

'And why is that, Thora?'

'These sound like trick questions to me.' Thora frowned, scratching her elbows. 'I guess it's because I've been very busy.'

'Busy doing what?'

'"Living between worlds" is how my mother puts it.'

'Stop talking rubbish,' said Mrs Grubb impatiently.

'Mr Walters says that I'll probably have to attend school eventually, but that the first five or six years are a complete waste of time anyway. He's always said I have learned much more from reading books and travelling than I ever would from sitting in alphabetical order in a mouldy old classroom.'

Mr Mason laced his fingers together and put his hands on his chest. 'Is Mr Walters a qualified teacher?'

'Oh, no. He would never become a teacher. He is a *man of the world.*'

'But you can read, I presume?'

'Oh, yes. Mr Walters taught me when I was four.'

'What sort of books?'

'Oh, you know, whatever Mr Walters managed to have air-lifted to the *Loki.*'

'Such as?'

'Let's see. *The Annotated Biography of Donald Bradman,* the cricketer, was a good one. I also enjoyed *Njal's Saga.*'

'Njal's what?'

'Saga. It's set in medieval Iceland – a ripping tale! The chieftain, Njal, was beardless – not like the hairy potter from Cape Town! Author unknown. It's quite an olden-time story, though not as olden-time as the Bible. What else? Let me see ...'

Mr Mason changed tack. 'Travel and reading are fine and good,' he said, 'but school teaches you things like mathematics.'

'What, like quadratic equations and calculus?'

'Well, we start with arithmetic and move on to those when you are older.'

'What's the point of going backwards? It would be a shame to unlearn what I know already. And a lot of work to learn it again!'

Mr Mason tried another new slant. 'In the classroom you will learn discipline.'

'My mother taught me that when she swam the lakes and rivers of the world.'

'And manners.'

Thora bowed, a three-quarter bow that she had been taught in Tokyo. 'Did you know that in Japan it is considered rude to smile at a stranger?' She paused. 'One thing that does interest me about school ...'

'Yes?' said Mr Mason.

'It's something I read about in *Anne of Green Gables*. Does each student really get a *slate* to write on? Do you remember the way she hit Gilbert Blythe over the head with her slate because he called her "carrots"? I'd do the same, I think, though I would have forgiven him faster than Anne. She was a proud old thing. But you often see that in red-haired people – have you noticed?'

'We've moved on from then,' said Mr Mason. 'Our students use pens and paper.'

'Fountain pens with silver nibs that you dip in black inkwells? Mr Walters uses Sir Josiah Mason 1002 Fine Point. They're quite hard to get hold of. He's only been able to find them at the Royal College of Art in London. He calls it The Great World Nib Shortage.'

'*Ballpoint* pens.'

'That's too bad,' said Thora. 'They blot when you carry them in your pocket.'

'I think school will do this girl a world of good,' said Mr Mason to Mrs Grubb. 'She'll learn to be quiet and respectful. And she'll study proper subjects like social studies and science.'

'It's so strange when people talk about you as if you're not there!' observed Thora aloud. 'But perhaps that is one of the customs around here. One never knows exactly how to judge these matters. Each country is so very different.'

'What is your surname, Thora?'

'Surname? I don't think I have one.'

'That's nonsense. Everyone has a last name. What was your father's surname?'

'My father died before I was even born,' Thora said slowly. 'And my mother never found it out, because it wasn't part of her culture to have a family name. What about a surname from *Njal's Saga*? Those characters had rather interesting last names. You can call me Thora Mord Fiddle if you like.'

Mr Mason sighed. 'That will do for now, Thora. You will start in Mr Butterfield's class in one month's time. On your first day of class, please report to Room Four wearing the regulation blue and white checked uniform that I understand Mrs Grubb has generously purchased for you with her own money. I would also like you to wear proper shoes on your feet.'

'I'm sorry, that's out of the question.'

'Why is that?'

'My second toe is much longer than my big toe. Regular shoes don't fit.'

Mr Mason looked down at Thora's feet. 'We don't let our students wear windsurfing slippers to class.'

Mrs Grubb whispered something into Mr Mason's ear.

'*Diam Rem?*' said Mr Mason. 'Never heard of it. I'd like her to have a proper medical check-up too.'

Thora shrugged. 'Not all doctors are familiar with the condition.'

Mr Mason sighed. 'I think we'll skip the tour of the school, Mrs Grubb. Good day.'

Chapter 35

The town was small, and so they didn't have to walk far before they came to the Rukle residence, a house badly in need of a paint job. There was a swing set and a sand box and a toy schoolhouse about the size of an orange crate, and off to one side, a badminton net. Thora's foster parents were waiting behind a gate with a sign nearby.

BEWARE of DOG.

In a flash, Thora realised she'd seen them before.

The pale, red-eyed Mrs Rukle was the woman she'd seen sobbing on the beach the night of the storm.

And the fat man was the bully who'd grabbed Ricky by the scruff of the neck on the pier – she'd seen him at the Tooty Frooty, too, playing the slot machines.

As she followed the couple up the walkway, the tough little dog that Ricky had called Tiny Stevens began to bark. The door slammed and two children emerged from the house.

Ricky laughed when he saw Thora. 'You!' he said, looking down at her feet.

'Thora, meet your new brother and sister,' said Mrs Grubb. 'Ricky and Lynne. Now, you children run off and play while I finalise the paperwork.'

The children were grateful to be released.

'I can't believe it's *you!*' said Ricky. 'I never told them, just like you asked ... well, except for Lynne. The coast guard said I was really lucky. They'd never seen the wind die down so suddenly. It was practically *supernatural.*'

'Are you a witch?' asked Lynne, chewing at a fingernail. She had pale blonde hair cut in a straight fringe above her glasses, and her feet were bare. 'Can I see your feet?'

'Maybe later,' said Thora. 'Now, what do we have here?'

They showed Thora their toys. The swing was too small for her. The badminton rackets were coming unstrung, and the posts holding up the badminton net were rotten and fell over when she tapped them. Although it all looked cheerful from a distance, the sad truth was that everything was falling apart. Even the little toy schoolhouse was blackened on one side where someone had tried to set it on fire.

'We set it all up this morning for you,' said Ricky. 'Normally Dad says toys are for spoiled brats.'

'We found it all at the rubbish dump,' said Lynne.

The children explained to Thora that the family was very poor. Mr Rukle had lost all his money at the Tooty Frooty. He was addicted to the slot machines. 'Mum feels tired all the time and has to have long rests on the couch. Mr and Mrs Grubb are going to give us money to take care of you.'

'That's nice. How much?' asked Thora.

'Enough to make it worthwhile,' said Lynne.

Thora picked up the schoolhouse and held it over her head. 'Let's take this garbage back to where it belongs.'

Ricky smiled. 'We don't like these toys anyway.'

'They don't even work,' said Lynne.

'They're no fun,' said Ricky.

'Of course not,' said Thora. 'You know why?'

'Why?' asked Lynne.

'Because they were made by grown-ups. Now, if it was up to children, there wouldn't be these sorts of toys. No more plastic teacups and doll's houses and fake tool boxes and stupid electronic cars and walking animals that need double-A batteries. No more Junior Scrabble and miniature badminton sets that break after the first game and furry little animals made out of nylon. Why, when there are proper hammers, and games with rules that make sense, and real live cuddly furry warm animals that can sleep on your bed with you at night?'

She threw the schoolhouse up into the air and Ricky caught it.

'Why have a plastic school when you live down the street from a real one?' She pointed and broke into a trot. 'C'mon!'

The children followed Thora into the school playground. Thora opened an unlocked window and they sneaked inside.

'This is the best way to go to school,' said Thora. 'When you're not supposed to!'

The room they found themselves in was quiet. The smell of chalk and gym shoes hung in the air. They examined the large map of the world on the wall. Thora rifled through the teacher's desk and found some bright yellow highlighters. 'Let's each

mark where in the world we've been.'

Ricky and Lynne found the area where Grimli was and Thora coloured it yellow.

'Now, where else?'

Ricky and Lynne looked at each other. 'Our grandmother is from Woking,' said Lynne.

'But we've never been there,' said Ricky. 'Or anywhere else.'

Thora looked at them in astonishment. 'How dreadful!' she said. 'Then why not colour in all the places where you'd *like* to go?'

'I'd like to join the circus,' said Lynne.

'OK,' said Thora, colouring in Russia. 'There is an

excellent circus in Moscow, which has people who can tie themselves in knots and men who can be shot out of a canon through rings of fire into the jaws of hippopotamuses.'

Lynne smiled. 'Oh yes, let's go to Russia! Like Eloise in *Eloise in Moscow*!'

'Yes,' said Thora. 'She had a good life full of travel and adventure – though she didn't get to see much of her mother.'

'That would be horrible,' said Lynne.

'It depends, I guess,' said Thora thoughtfully.

It was Ricky's turn. He looked dreamily out of the window. 'I want to go to the Rock,' he said.

'That's *so* boring,' said Lynne. 'Thora means a real place. Out in the world.'

'The Rock *is* a real place,' said Ricky.

'OK,' said Thora, 'but it's not marked on the map. Where else do you want to go?'

He thought for a while. 'Someplace to swim with dolphins.'

'Righty-o,' said Thora. 'We've got a few options for that. How about Zanzibar? After the dolphins you can have a fruit fight with a monkey. *Jambo, jambo!* And chase pot-bellied pigs and eat chicken satay with peanut sauce! Yum!'

They heard a crackle, and from a speaker over the clock, a voice. 'Who's there?'

'Time to split,' whispered Thora. 'Shhh.'

Lynne began to chew her fingernails. 'That's the headteacher, Mr Mason. He'll beat us with the Board of Education.'

'I'll tan his hide if he tries such a thing,' said Thora, indignantly.

Their voices were drowned out by the sound of a burglar alarm.

They slipped back out through the window and into the playground. They ran as fast as they could to the fence. Thora helped the other two over and tossed them the toy schoolhouse, then climbed over herself.

'Stop running,' said Thora. 'Walk. Be casual.'

Just then a police car turned into the street. It was heading for the school! Thora waved.

'What are you doing?' whispered Ricky, frightened.

The car slowed down and the policeman peered out at them. 'You know anything about this business with the school?' he asked, suspiciously.

'Absolutely,' nodded Thora. 'Someone's tried to set it on fire. Luckily, the damage is minimal. In fact, one hardly notices it. I say, officer, why don't you ride a horse like your good colleague?'

The policeman frowned, ignoring her last remark. 'Fire?'

'Yes,' she said, pointing out the burned side of the plastic schoolhouse. 'Could you suggest where we should take it for repairs? Actually,' she added, 'we've outgrown it – but some younger child might find it amusing.'

'I've got a little boy, two years old, who would like it,' said the policeman. He looked over to the real building, relieved that she was only talking about a toy. 'I'll buy it from you. For five pounds.'

Thora let her hair fall into her face. 'Fifteen,' she said. 'Not including delivery.'

They settled on ten. Thora gave five to Ricky and five to Lynne.

'Put it in the boot and I'll drive you home.'

'Oh, yes!' cried Ricky. 'A ride in a real live cop car!'

The policeman let them look at his radio and touch some of the important-looking buttons. He even took them on a little detour through town. As he drove, he told them that he had always wanted to be a policeman.

'It's nice when dreams come true!' sang Thora.

Finally, his radio beeped and a crackly voice said, 'Where the dickens are you? We're waiting for you on that B&E over at the school. Over.'

'What's that?' said Thora.

'Break and enter,' said the policeman. He dropped them home and sped off, siren blaring.

Chapter 36

Mr Rukle was waiting on the steps. He had removed his jacket and wore a grimy grey shirt with big sweat stains under the armpits. His face was purple. Big veins pulsed on his temple like a frog's heart beat. 'What have you been up to now?' he said. 'No lies.'

'We've been having a wonderful time,' said Thora.

'With that copper? What sort of trouble are you in? Git inside, the three of you.'

The children darted into the house and through to the kitchen, where Ricky and Lynne stood staring at the floor.

Thora did a cartwheel. *Smuch!* went her windsurfing slippers. 'We were only away for fifteen minutes,' she said, checking her watch. 'Then the policeman gave us a ride home. He was a nice chap, wasn't he, Lynne? Hey, where's Mrs Grubb?'

'Shuddup. She got fed up with waiting for you.' He pointed his sausage finger so close to Thora's face that she had to cross her eyes to follow it. 'She needs you to sign some form before she can give us the money. She had to rush off to get to some fancy dinner at the Tooty Frooty. So we still haven't been paid.'

He swung around to glare at Lynne and Ricky. 'Whaddya staring at? Hey! What's that?' He tore the five-pound note out of Lynne's hand. 'Did you steal it? I should've guessed. Go to the Punishment Room. And you, Ricky, go and chop some wood.' He cuffed him on the ear.

'Ouch!' shouted Ricky.

'Shuddup. Your mother has a headache. Time to start thinking about other people for once in your lives.' He turned to Thora. 'And you!' he shouted, nose hairs dancing. 'I think we need to get a few things straight around here.'

'Yes, we do,' said Thora, fascinated. 'Such as, why are you performing the *haka* without a grass skirt?'

From the stairs, Lynne gasped.

Mr Rukle spluttered.

'I thought all Maori dancers wore grass skirts. I may not be remembering correctly, though, as I was only very tiny when my mother swam the Great Bear River near Wellington.'

'Button your lip, missy, or I'll do it for you!'

Thora laughed heartily. 'Good one! *Button your lip*. That's one of the things I just *love* about living in a new place. All the unique vertinacular expressions you come across. I wonder if that phrase translates well into Russian. Lynne will find out when she goes to see the circus in Moscow!'

Lynne rushed up the stairs into the Punishment Room.

'Get over here, girl,' said Mr Rukle to Thora, rolling up his sleeves. 'It's time to teach you a lesson.'

'Oh, no, thanks. I'd rather do the *haka*. The All Blacks do it before their football games.' She leaned forward and made her eyes pop and grunted and stuck out her tongue in the style of Maori dancers.

'*Ugug, ughughuggugug!*'

Mrs Rukle peeked into the kitchen. Mr Rukle's back was turned, so he didn't see her, and that was lucky, because she was smiling. She suddenly looked quite pretty. Then she disappeared again.

'Do the haka!' shouted Thora.

Mr Rukle stamped his feet and waved his arms and the purple veins on his temples wiggled and danced. The five pounds he had taken from Lynne sailed to the floor.

'That's the way!' cheered Thora, scooping up the note.

He grabbed her ponytail, but she yanked it out of his hand, limbo-danced under his arm and scampered up on to the kitchen table. '*Ugugugu, ugmugga, BOO!*'

'I'm gonna get you!' he cried furiously.

Thora threw open the window and slipped out into the back yard. '*Pssss!*' she said, looking up at the window on the first floor. 'Lynne!' Lynne opened the window. Thora removed the box containing the little lava statue of Neptune from her pocket, wrapped it in the five-pound note using an elastic band, and tossed it up into Lynne's outstretched hand.

'It won't pay for your journey to Moscow, but every little bit helps!'

'Bye, Thora!'

'Cheerio!' waved Thora. 'Send me a postcard from the circus!'

Chapter 37

Two weeks later, on a lazy Thursday afternoon, as Thora was painting a picture of a sea dragon on her bedroom wall and pondering whether sea dragons had belly buttons, she heard the *bzzzz* and *whirllll* of Frooty de Mare's plane landing once again in the harbour.

'The de Mares are back, Cosmo,' she said, rinsing her paintbrush in a cup of cold tea.

A knock came on the door.

'Hello there! Come on in!'

Holly handed her a glossy flyer. 'Can't. I'm delivering promotional material for my dad's business.'

Thora looked down at the sheet.

'New cinema?' she said. 'Grimli already *has* a cinema.'

'I know,' said Holly. 'But the Allbent Cinema is very out-of-date. My dad's cinema will be much nicer. And he'll show better films.'

Thora considered this. 'The more the merrier!' she said. 'I'll come to the opening! But it's tomorrow night. Could I have a few extra flyers? I'd like to give one to the Rukles.'

Holly looked surprised. 'You know the Rukles?'

'Yep. I almost moved in with them.'

'They used to be my best friends,' said Holly.

'Used to be? How sad,' said Thora.

'My dad says they're rough and common and that they're going nowhere fast.'

Thora remembered how Ricky and Lynne had told her that Mr Rukle had lost all his money on the slot machines. She'd even seen him playing the machines herself.

'Oh no,' said Thora. 'They've got big plans. In fact, Lynne is going to Moscow and Ricky is considering Zanzibar.'

Once again, she invited Holly on to the *Loki*.

'You don't know how *desolate* it's been,' said Thora. 'Since Mr Walters left it feels like I've barely spoken *two words*. Cosmo is good company most of the time – but at other times he's just so into himself. By the way, I'm Thora.'

'Holly de Mare.'

Thora's eyes widened. 'Well, why didn't you say so before? What a beautiful name! *Holly*. My mother used to wear a wreath of holly around her neck as a necklace. Only at Christmas time, of course.'

Holly smiled and revealed two dimples in each cheek.

'The fact is, holly berries are extremely poisonous,' said Thora.

The dimples vanished. 'No, they're not.'

'Yes, they are. I knew of a Greenlandic princess who

thought they were so beautiful that she ate an entire bowl of them. With cream and sugar. God rest her soul.'

'She died?'

'Dead as a doornail. She didn't even have the fortitude to write out a will.'

'Her poor parents!'

Thora tapped Holly's shoulder. 'See what my ma bequeathed to me?' She did a twirl and the medals around her waist clanged together.

'Your mother has ... passed away?'

'Course not,' said Thora.

'Then where is she?' asked Holly, looking around for signs of a mother.

'It's a long story,' said Thora. 'Let's just say she's away for a while ... swimming.'

'Swimming? Why?'

'Why not?'

'Where?'

'Where do you think!' exclaimed Thora, pointing to the water all around them.

Holly started to look worried. 'I have to go. I'll get in trouble if these aren't delivered.'

'It's up to you,' said Thora, popping a cod cheek into her mouth.

Holly hesitated. She had never met a girl like Thora before. 'Did that girl who died have a funeral or anything?'

'Well ...' said Thora, 'as she drew her last breath, the

146

girl whispered this in my ear: "Thora! Beware of the red holly berry!" Then the pallor of death rose in her cheeks and a trickle of scarlet blood ran out the side of her mouth. And she *died*. It was an epical tragedy. She was a brave soul.'

'How terrible,' managed Holly. 'What did her mother and father do after that?'

'Well, now the story gets interesting. They wanted to bury her, of course.'

Holly nodded.

'But the earth was too frozen to manage this. Permafrost, you see. Three metres down. The ground never thaws in the Arctic. Digging was out of the question. And so they placed the girl on an iceberg and let her float away to Heaven.'

'Terrible!'

'Oh, not at all. It was very romantic. They gave her a terrific send-off. Everyone in town came. They covered her with a caribou skin and a Hudson Bay blanket. Then they protected her spirit with a little fence of whale teeth. She was really very comfortable. But the best part is this: as she floated away, a baby seal jumped up on her iceberg and tickled her with his whiskers. And the girl woke up!'

Holly brightened. 'She didn't die?'

'Not in the end, thanks to the seal. Seals are a lot of fun. They swim upside down.'

'They do?'

'Yes, siree!'

'Why?'

'Why? Because it's *fun*! Why don't you give it a whirl?'

Holly folded her arms across her chest. 'You're making this whole story up. I don't believe you. Not a word!'

'Well ... she *did* get sick on the berries.' Thora shrugged.

Holly's cheeks reddened. 'It's wicked to tell lies.'

'I've said nothing that didn't almost sort of happen.'

'You've made *everything* up.'

'Well, *my mother* likes my stories. They kept her awake as she swam the lakes and rivers of the world. Swimming can be so boring. Sometimes my mother fell asleep as she swam and I had to SHOUT STORIES AT HER LIKE THIS. She always needed to know what happened next. Don't *you* need to know?'

While Holly was thinking about Thora's question, Thora asked another. 'Do you want to come to the cinema with me tonight?'

'Oh, yes!' answered Holly immediately. Then her face fell. 'But I can't. Not to the Allbent. And anyway, my dad's cinema opens tomorrow night. Then I can go to as many films as I like.'

'Why can't you go to the Allbent?'

'It's a family rule. My dad is feuding with the Greenberg sisters.'

'Rules are made to be broken,' said Thora, 'or at least bent. No harm in asking. Let's go beg.'

chapter 38

Thora wanted to make a good impression on Holly's parents and so she asked Holly to wait a moment.

She went off to her room and hauled out the tea chest from under the bed to hunt for a gift for the de Mares. A snorkel? A fish bone? A gold medal? Hmmm. Then she saw an ancient set of yellow teeth. 'They're a little dirty,' she said, sashaying into the main room, 'but what do you expect from a scurvy old pirate?'

She linked arms with Holly and they set off.

'I'm not sure this is a good idea,' said Holly.

'Scared, are you?' Thora patted Holly on the back. 'I was scared once, too.'

'When?'

'Oh, just last year, after my mother swam the Juan de Fuca Strait. I went for a long walk on the beach and the sun went down. I had to turn back in the dark. It was completely black. No moon. Suddenly, the beach began to rustle. I took a step, and something crackled under my foot and squeezed up through my toes. And I had to walk at least a kilometre back down the beach.'

'What was it that crackled?'

'Sea crabs. They come out each night and cover the beach. I would have just swum back, but I figured it was easier for me to step on them than swim through them.'

Holly shivered.

'Aw, they were harmless. I do feel bad now about the ones I squashed, though.'

They paused for a moment outside the de Mares' cabin cruiser.

'Don't be scared,' said Thora.

Chapter 39

The living room of the cabin cruiser resembled the lobby of the Tooty Frooty. The walls were gold and the carpet was purple. The three de Mare brothers lay on the floor before a huge television screen.

'It smells like sea cow in here!' exclaimed Thora.

Holly pointed to a mountain of sneakers and held her nose.

Thora nodded. 'Do they ever wash?'

'Never,' said Holly.

'Do they speak?'

'Not much,' said Holly.

'Why the red polka dots on their faces?'

'Shhhh!' said Holly. Then she whispered into Thora's ear. 'They're pimples! Mummy says that they get them from my dad's family. They stand in the mirror and squeeze them. I've seen them pop!'

Mermaids did not get pimples. Thora was intrigued.

'Excuse me,' she said, poking one of the brothers. 'Is it true that if you squeeze a pinkle it will pop?'

Three heads turned.

'Oh look! You've *all* got pinkles! It's very festive! Why do you want to pop them?'

They grunted and turned back to watch the television.

Thora walked over and turned it off. 'Televisions have the ability to hypnotise even the nicest people!'

The brothers stared at Thora. Nobody had ever *dared* to interrupt Thursday boxing. Not even their father would chance it!

'You're just like all the zombies playing the slot machines down at the Tooty Frooty!' she remarked, conversationally.

The biggest brother beat his chest and farted. The other two belched.

Then all at once, the three of them rose to their feet and surrounded her.

Darting out of their way, Thora pulled a gold medal from the chain around her waist and held it up. *'You are getting very sleepy,'* she said.

She had never tried to hypnotise anyone before. But she had seen Boris the Remarkable at the Monterey Bay Sea Show and now she copied his technique. 'I want you all to look at this medal. You are beginning to feel very sleepy. Your eyes are heavy.'

She spoke in a low, soothing voice and let the medal swing back and forth.

Six small brown eyes followed it.

Six eyes began to droop.

Six eyes closed.

'Now, when I clap my hands you will all think you are ... apes. Gorillas, to be more exact. Shy yet sociable creatures. *Very* clean!'

She clapped her hands.

The boys began to grunt in a nice way. Then they smoothed the pillows on the sofa, seated themselves in a neat row and began to check each other's heads for nits.

'Gorillas?' said Holly, her eyes wide.

'Gorillas are actually very nice primates,' said Thora. 'Grooming is their favourite activity – they can do it *all day long!*' She saw a comb resting on a table and she passed it to them.

Holly giggled. 'Mummy's been trying to get them to do that for their whole lives!' She rushed out of the room and returned with a bottle of perfume and some lipstick. 'This will keep them busy for a while!'

The boys removed the stopper from the bottle and took turns dousing each other. The air filled with the scent of wild magnolias. Thora sneezed. 'My word!' she said. 'It reminds me of the open swimming awards ceremony at the Four Seasons Hotel in Tripoli! Mother and I were rushed to the hospital with perfume poisoning!'

Mrs de Mare bustled into the room. 'It's very strange,' she said, snapping on an earring, 'but my favourite perfume has disappeared! The very expensive bottle that Daddy bought me in Paris.'

A funny look came over her face.

'I'm afraid it's the lunkheads,' said Thora.

The perfume bottle lay on the floor, empty. They had moved on to the lipstick. One son was applying it in thick red stripes to another's lips. They reeked of wild magnolias.

Mrs de Mare gasped and fell backwards in a dead faint.

At that moment, the high whine of a speedboat could be heard outside. A few seconds later, the clatter of footsteps.

'Ooh!' said Holly.

The door burst open and her father staggered in.

She shrieked.

Frooty was wearing his leather coat, but it was torn and wet and dripping with seaweed.

His face was puffed and bloody and one eye had swollen shut. He was extremely happy.

He pointed to his wife, lying on the floor. 'What's the matter with her?'

'She fainted!' sang Thora.

Mrs de Mare began to groan. 'Where am I?' She opened her eyes and gazed up at her husband.

'You're right here, Pussy-chops,' he said. 'Everything's all right.' He smiled broadly.

Mrs de Mare sat bolt upright. 'Where are your two front teeth?'

Frooty had already been a little scary-looking. But toothless, with one black eye and a bloodied face, he looked positively gruesome. He attempted to help his wife to her feet but she smacked him away.

'What's happened?' asked Holly timidly.

'A miracle!' said Frooty. 'The answer to all our prayers. The reward for all my labours. A marvellous and magical thing has occurred.' He gazed up at the ceiling, hugging himself in delight. 'The opening of the cinema tomorrow night is going to be fantastic!'

Everyone waited for him to finish. Even the boys looked over.

'But I can't tell you about it, tweety birds. Not yet.'

'Well, how miraculous can it be if it's knocked out your two front teeth? Go look at yourself!' said Mrs de Mare, furious. 'How can we go out for dinner with you looking like a ...'

'Pirate?' finished Thora helpfully. With a flourish, she held up the gift she had brought. 'Here are some real pirate teeth.'

Chapter 40

'Who is this ... *creature?*' asked Mrs de Mare, aghast.

'The name is Thora.'

Frooty was lost in his own world. He inspected himself in the mirror. 'Hmmm. Not good.' He turned around. 'Did you say *teeth?*'

'Pirate teeth,' said Thora. 'My mother found them off the coast of the Philippines, near Myanmar. The great granddaughter of King Thibaw assured us that they were the real thing.'

Frooty held them up to the light. 'Whalebone?' he asked, impressed.

'Yep!' said Thora. 'Try them on!'

'No,' said Mrs de Mare firmly. 'He will go to a proper dentist.'

'I will do no such thing,' said Frooty.

'Daddy hates dentists,' explained Holly.

'Take a seat and say, *"Ahhhh"*,' said Thora.

'Ahhhhh ...'

'They fit!' she announced briskly. 'Just like Cinderella's slipper!' Then she pulled out the little cloth that she used to collect her mermaid drips and wiped Frooty's coat. 'All you need now is an eye patch and Bob's your uncle!'

Frooty frowned. Holly had never brought home a friend like Thora. She was a strange girl. And oddly dressed. There was something, well ... *fishy* about her.

'Hey!' he suddenly exclaimed, snapping his fingers. 'Haven't I met you before?'

'Yep.'

'You're the girl who said rude things about my stuffed mermaid!'

'That would be me,' said Thora.

'Well, have I got a big surprise for you!' said Frooty laughing softly. 'Now how much do I owe you for the teeth?'

'Parts and labour are free,' replied Thora. 'But there is one small favour I would like to ask.'

'Ask away.'

'It won't cost much.'

'Then I'm sure it can be arranged.'

'Two tickets to the Allbent tonight. For Holly and me.'

The room fell silent. 'No,' he said firmly. 'You can go to my cinema when it opens tomorrow night.'

'But you just said ...' Holly plunged her face into her hands.

'The answer is *no*, you silly girl! And anyway, I don't know why you want to go to that revolting place when we have a perfectly good television set *right here*.' He pulled out a fifty-pound note. 'Here. Take this. Go and buy yourselves a pizza or something. Rent a video. Have a nice time.'

'What a wonderful idea!' said Mrs de Mare brightly. 'Aren't you lucky girls? You'll have a lovely time, I'm sure.'

Chapter 41

The two girls waved goodbye and set off. It was a cool evening, with the smell of burning leaves in the air.

'I'm sorry I can't go to the Allbent,' said Holly.

'Oh, you'll get there one day, I'm sure. I can feel it in my scales.'

'Your scales?'

'Why doesn't your father like the Greenberg sisters, anyway?' Thora asked quickly, changing the subject.

'Because they won't sell him the cinema. It sits on prime real estate, you know.'

'It's a beautiful old building,' said Thora.

'Oh, Daddy doesn't care about *that*. He'd tear it down and build a new one.'

They walked on for a few minutes in silence.

'There's nothing to do here,' sighed Holly. 'If we were in the city we could go to my aunty's house and play with her wigs and make-up. This town is *so* boring.'

'Boring? This place?' To brighten Holly's mood, Thora did a cartwheel. 'Ever tried to watch seaweed grow? Or take a time-lapse photo of a melting Finnish iceberg?'

Holly shook her head.

'They're *very* boring.' She scratched her elbow. 'I have an idea. Let's have a birthday party!'

'For who?

'For us.'

'It's not my birthday. Is it yours?'

'Nope. But it was – and it will be again.'

Holly gave this idea some thought. 'We could dress up.'

'And bake a birthday cake!'

'And sprinkle it with hundreds and thousands.'

'Hundreds and thousands of what?'

Holly laughed. 'Hundreds and thousands of *hundreds and thousands*!'

They paused in front of the all-night supermarket, The Tombody. 'Maybe we should buy our birthday supplies in here,' said Holly, dragging Thora in by the hand.

The supermarket was almost empty, but the aisles were well lit. They were full of foods that seemed strange to Thora. She rushed over to a section marked FROZEN FOODS. 'Look,' she said, perplexed, holding up a packet.

'Fish fingers,' said Holly. 'When we were small, that's all we would ever eat.'

'But fish don't have *fingers*,' said Thora. 'And if they did I certainly wouldn't want to eat them! And look over there. Rock cakes. How revolting.'

'Oh, no. Rock cakes are delicious,' said Holly.

'Thora!' came a voice.

Thora turned to see Ricky and Lynne running down the aisle towards them.

'What are you doing here?' asked Ricky.

'Getting supplies for our birthday party. Wanna come?'

'Oh, yes! Whose birthday is it?'

'Everybody's!'

Mrs Rukle appeared, pushing a loaded shopping cart. She no longer looked pale and tired. In fact, she looked very well. Her cheeks were tinged with pink and she had a nice new hairstyle.

'Hello, Thora,' she said, smiling. 'How are you?'

'All the better for seeing you!'

Ricky and Lynne asked their mother if they could join Thora's birthday celebration. She nodded. 'I'll pick you up in a couple of hours.'

'The more the merrier,' said Thora.

Ricky and Lynne were very excited and couldn't wait to tell Thora their wonderful news. Their mother had used the ten pounds from the policeman to pay for an appraisal of the statue of Neptune that Thora had given them.

'*That* funny old thing!' said Thora. 'I hope you scraped the lichen off it first!'

They had sold the object to a dealer at Sotheby's in London for a lot of money – enough to leave Mr Rukle and move into a new house on the other side of town!

And to pay for a wonderful second-hand car!

'Hurrah!' cried Thora.

When they found themselves in the FRESH FRUIT AND VEGETABLES section, Thora looked around. 'Hey, where's Holly?'

'Holly?'

'She was with me a minute ago.'

'Not Holly *de Mare*!' said Lynne.

'You mean Holly *de Nightmare*!' said Ricky.

'How odd,' said Thora.

'She *is* odd.'

'Don't you like her?' asked Thora, puzzled.

'We *used* to like her,' said Ricky.

'Good! Then it will take no time at all for you to like her again.'

They retraced their steps and found Holly crouching in the INTERNATIONAL FOODS aisle under a sign advertising instant cappuccino.

'I found some of your old friends,' said Thora. 'Isn't it a small world! Like a connect-the-dots puzzle.'

Holly took a deep breath. Then she whispered in Thora's ear: 'They don't like me. They think I'm stuck up.'

'Stuck up?' asked Thora. 'Stuck up *what*?'

Lynne and Ricky folded their arms on their chests and looked away.

'Nobody is stuck up *anything*, as far as I can see,' said Thora cheerfully. 'Except that lady on the ladder. Hey, ma'am, is this where I'll find a tub of gentlemen's relish?'

The woman shook her head. 'Never heard of it.'

'What about gefilte fish?'

'Gefilte what?'

'Skyr?'

'Are you having me on?'

'Jeepers,' whispered Thora. 'They're not very well stocked. Let's go back to the *Loki*. The larder there is full already. I'll make an angel food cake and we'll get the party started.'

Chapter 42

It was an altogether bleak autumn evening, with sky and sea the colour of wet cement, and yet the air seemed to crackle with excitement.

'Come in, come in!' said Thora, swinging the door of the *Loki* wide open. 'If I'd had more warning, I would have vacuumed the Turkish carpet.' She raided the cupboards and set out some treats. Then they played games.

Each had their own idea of the sorts of things they should do to celebrate everybody's birthday. Lynne wanted to play Musical Chairs, but there weren't enough chairs. So they played Pin the Tail on the Peacock. But Cosmo didn't like that game. So they tried bobbing for apples. But Thora could stay underwater for such a long time that it wasn't much of a contest. Holly wanted to dress up. Thora handed her an old Halla-Skin. Ricky donned one of

Mr Walters' old trilby hats. Lynne found a matador's vest that Halla had been awarded in Pamplona.

Finally, Thora announced that she would make the birthday cake. While she busied herself in the kitchen, the others feasted on cucumber sandwiches and miniature gherkins. When they got thirsty, Thora poured them long glasses of tonic water. 'Nothing like it to quench a desert thirst.' She stirred in scoops of vanilla ice cream to remove the bitterness and brightened the whole thing up with slices of canned beetroot.

While the cake baked, Thora suggested they take a little boat ride.

'Yippee!' shouted Ricky.

Soon they were sailing through the harbour and into the open sea. It was a cold, moonless, breathless, starless night.

The sea stretched on forever like dark wrinkled velvet.

'I'm scared,' said Holly.

'There's no one by that name in here!' sang Thora, producing from the oven a slightly sunken angel food cake. 'No matter, we'll build it up again with whipped cream and candles and nobody will know the difference.'

They sang 'Happy Birthday' and blew out the candles and tucked into their cake.

'Ouch!' cried Holly, leaping up. 'I've bitten something hard!'

'Phew,' said Thora. 'I was worried you might swallow it.'

Holly held up a small white pearl. She nibbled it. 'Is it real?'

'What other kind of pearl is there?'

'I might have choked!' said Holly. 'Why did you put it in?'

'I put in dozens of them. I wanted to make a polka-dot cake but there weren't any polka dots left and we were clear out of confetti.'

'I've got one too!' cried Lynne.

'You'll each have a handful before the cake is finished,' said Thora. 'Keep them. They make good substitutes for marbles.'

She got up and put one of Mr Walters' records on the record player. 'Strangers in the Night' swirled through the cabin.

'And now for the main attraction.' She peeled away the Turkish carpet to reveal, on the floor, the great round dark window to the sea.

'What on earth is it?' asked Holly.

'What *in sea*, you mean.' Thora pressed a red button. 'Come and look for yourselves!'

A great cone of light stretched from the floor of the *Loki* all the way down to the dark floor of the sea.

A distance of 2.5 kilometres!

There was a dazzled hush.

There were small fish that looked like pink beetles and large fish that resembled electric handsaws. There were blowfish and eels and sea cows. And there were a thousand flickering shadows on the sea floor.

Two octopuses swam into the column of light holding sticks. They began to joust.

'Squid pro quo,' said Thora, waving. 'They owed me a favour!'

A group of pot-bellied sea horses swam through the column.

'My mother knew a mer-dwarf who grew up on a sea-horse ranch,' said Thora. 'She used to ride her sea horse, Simon, to school every day. When Simon had a baby, it was only six millimetres long! They named it Yves. It ate 3600 shrimp every day!'

'Simon had a baby?' asked Ricky, puzzled.

'Yep! The boys have the babies.'

'I'm glad I'm not a sea horse,' said Ricky, puzzled.

It was then that a mermaid passed through the cone of light.

With eight eyes peering down at her, it was no wonder she looked startled.

She swam several circles around the cone. Holding her body in the shadow, she stared up at them. Her eyes were large and rather bloodshot, her hair a floating frame of yellow. She waved uncertainly.

'It's a mermaid! It's too bright for her,' said Holly. 'Can you soften the lights?'

The mermaid looked very upset.

'She's trying to tell you something, Thora!' cried Lynne.

Thora forgot all about being undercover. She got down on her hands and knees and pressed her ear to the glass.

'What is she saying, Thora?' asked Holly.

'Shush!' said Thora.

'Wow,' breathed Ricky. 'Thora can understand her!'

'Didn't you hear what Thora said?' hissed Lynne. 'Be quiet!'

When Thora finally stood up there was a strange expression on her face.

Holly gazed down into the cone of light. The mermaid had fled. 'Where did she go? What's wrong, Thora? What did she say to you?'

Thora scratched hard at her elbows.

Holly stamped her foot. 'Aren't you going to tell us what is going on?'

'Why do you want to know?' said Thora, wringing her hands.

'What is it?' asked Lynne softly.

Thora decided she could confide in them. 'My mother lives on the Rock, but no one has seen her there for hours,' she whispered. 'I must try to find her.'

Soon the weight of that cement-coloured autumn sky made itself felt. The children's excitement had turned to fear.

Chapter 43

Everybody was planning to attend the opening of Frooty's new cinema.

The mayor, Grimus Grubb, and his wife Honey. The Chief of Police. The officer who bought the schoolhouse. The estate agent. The school headteacher, Mr Mason. The owners of the Tombody supermarket. The baker at Gulli's Goodies. The fishmonger. The taxi-cab driver. Even Mrs Valihora, the landlady from the now-demolished Blue Bell Bed and Breakfast.

Anybody who was anybody, and everybody else as well. The special guests received personal invitations in the mail; the rest found flyers stuffed in their letterboxes.

Some were going because they wanted to be seen. Some in order to see. Many were going in order to eat as many onion rings and popcorn balls as they could. Free of charge.

And *everybody* was curious to see Frooty's 'Big Surprise'.
YOU WON'T BELIEVE YOUR EYES.

It had been a very long time since something fun had
occurred in this sleepy seaside town. The air was electric.
Frooty was not exactly popular in Grimli. But you had to
hand it to him. He knew how to throw a party.

Mrs Grubb brought out her furs.

The Chief of Police polished his boots.

Mrs Rukle booked another appointment at the hair

stylist. And Mr Rukle laid out a clean shirt. He even thought about scraping the dirt from under his fingernails with an old carving knife. He hadn't eaten a proper meal since Mrs Rukle left and the thought of all that free food made his mouth water.

Only the Greenberg sisters had been excluded.

A large neon sign had been placed near the entrance of the new cinema. In bold orange neon lights it read BANISHED.

And beneath it appeared the names *Flossie, Dottie* and *Lottie Greenberg*.

The sisters didn't want to go anyway. They dashed off a quick note explaining why.

MR DE MARE,

THERE IS NO WAY WE WOULD LOWER OURSELVES TO SET FOOT IN THE MERMAID CINEMA. NO SELF-RESPECTING FILM LOVER COULD STAND YOUR GROTESQUE TASTE IN FILMS. YOU CAN'T FOOL US. WE KNOW YOUR MOVIES HAVE BEEN PIRATED ILLEGALLY FROM LATE-NIGHT TELEVISION AND THAT YOUR CURTAINS AND CHAIR COVERINGS ARE MADE OUT OF POLYESTER (A HIGH FIRE DANGER!) AND THAT YOUR MARINE MURALS HAVE BEEN PAINTED DIRECTLY ON TO STYROFOAM WALLS. YOU COULDN'T PAY US TO WATCH ONE OF YOUR VULGAR MOVIES OR EAT ONE OF YOUR DISGUSTING POPCORN BALLS.

NOTHING YOU COULD DO WOULD AMAZE US.

SINCERELY,
LOTTIE, DOTTIE AND FLOSSIE GREENBERG.

P.S. WE WILL NEVER EVER EVER CLOSE THE ALLBENT CINEMA, SO DREAM ON.

Chapter 44

It was the morning of Frooty's cinema opening. Thora jumped out of bed and ran as fast as she could to the beach.

It was a mild, overcast day and the water should have felt warm. Instead, it was so icy that it took her breath away. Within seconds, her body felt numb and her teeth began to chatter.

Although the Rock was hidden in mist, she knew its exact latitude and longitude without really having to think. A smoke-coloured fog was rolling in and she felt the rip tugging at her as she swam. The swimming was hard going. She felt the water trying to rob her of her strength and purpose.

She had considered taking the *Loki* to the Rock the night before to look for her mother, but with all of her friends aboard she had decided against it. She wasn't entirely sure how Holly would react.

It had been midnight before she'd returned to the Grimli pier and waved goodbye to her anxious and confused friends. It had been far too late and too dark even for a half-mermaid to attempt the swim out to the Rock. And she hadn't taken the boat out, because she hadn't wanted to risk having it spotted by anybody.

She approached the Rock now from the north side, where the ramp was, and searched the edge for a toehold. Then she hoisted herself on to the slope and scrambled up, calling, 'MOTHER, WHERE ARE YOU?'

The mist was clearing, and now Thora could see quite plainly that she was alone.

Calming herself, she called to her mother once more.

Again, no reply.

A knife-edge of fear ran down her chest and legs and into her toes. She trembled – more from fear than cold. Something bad had happened, she knew.

She searched every millimetre of the Rock, careful not to tread on any of the pointy bits or slippery patches. She stepped sideways along the little rock ledge on the south side. Her eyes ran along the serrated edges, taking in the sea anemones, the dead crabs, the water beetles and rock spiders, the peaty pebbles and stunted grass. The tooth-like stones around the edges had taken on the appearance of fangs.

Each second felt like an eternity.

Just when she was giving up hope, her eye fell on a scattering of iridescent blue scales. She got down on her knees and examined them closely. They were Halla's, all right. There were handfuls of them. She followed the trail. It led her to the sharply plunging edge on the south side, and peering over it she saw that were were still more floating in the water below.

Sometimes Halla shed scales when she was grooming herself. Maybe it was nothing.

But then her eye fell on a clump of yellow between two wet rocks. With her heart pounding, she gathered it up, hoping that it might just be a clot of seaweed.

She inhaled.

It smelled of pumpkin pie.

At that moment, Frooty's plane passed overhead, a white banner streaming in its wake. The pilot seemed not to notice Thora. The plane did a series of somersaults. The white banner tumbled behind it and then flattened out enough for Thora to read its message.

TONIGHT'S THE NIGHT.
YOU WON'T BELIEVE YOUR EYES!

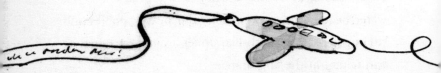

Chapter 45

They were all waiting for Thora on the deck of the *Loki* when she returned from the Rock. Holly, Ricky, Lynne and Cosmo. She climbed aboard and slipped into her windsurfing slippers. They made a sad *smuch! smuch!* sound as she walked toward her friends.

'Thora!' Holly threw both arms around her. 'Oh, I've been so worried! I've had the most terrible feeling that something bad has happened. Lynne and Ricky came by this morning when they couldn't find you on the *Loki*. Cosmo just shook his head when we asked where you were.'

'We thought you might have canoed out to the Rock,' said Ricky.

'You've been swimming,' said Lynne. 'Was she there?'

Thora's bottom lip quivered. She plunged her face into her hands.

'Whatever is wrong?' cried Holly. 'Oh, someone

please, pretty please, tell me what is going on!' She sat down beside Thora. 'Lynne and Ricky know something that I don't. They said you must tell me yourself. Please, Thora, tell me and let us help you!'

Ricky now approached Thora. 'Take off your slippers,' he said.

'Not on your life,' said Thora.

Ricky then leaned over and kissed her on the cheek.

Mr Walters had often kissed Thora on the cheek. But Ricky's kiss was something entirely different. Despite her terrible, wet, unhappy state, she felt the heat creep up her face in a very human blush.

'I think it will help her understand if she knows what you are,' he said.

Thora hesitated. She scratched both her elbows. Finally, she removed her shoes.

Holly stared at Thora's purple feet. Her long toes. Her scales.

'I'm half-mermaid,' explained Thora.

Everyone held their breath, waiting for Holly to either shriek in horror or begin to cry.

She did neither. Rather, she tucked her hair behind her ears and faced Thora squarely. She nodded matter-of-factly.

Her calm surprised Thora and encouraged her to go on. 'Remember what your father said the other night about a "big surprise"?'

Holly thought hard.

'He was all covered with seaweed, remember?'

The blood was draining from Holly's face. 'The marvellous, magical thing ...'

'Yes,' said Thora.

Outside, Cosmo was perched on the roof, his tail feathers hanging down the side of the cabin. He leaned over, his long blue neck stretching in Thora's direction and his eyes full of sympathy.

'My mother.'

Her words silenced the group.

Thora was not so sure that her friends could help her with a problem like this, but recalling what her mother had said as she bade Thora farewell on the Rock, she thought she might know who could.

Chapter 46

At the Allbent Cinema the lights were on but nobody answered her knock. She'd heard that the sisters had come back from Venice, but each time she'd dropped by Kat had told her to go away. Once she'd even chased her off with a broom.

Thora peered in. The blackboard was still there. Under the word BANISHED, two names. Frooty de Mare's and her own.

She waited, Cosmo standing loyally at her side, for what seemed a very long time. She was not sure how well her father had known the sisters. Only that he had worked at the cinema. She wondered if they would even remember him.

Eventually three figures, returning from their morning walk, crunched towards her across the gravel. Their noses and cheeks were rosy. They slowed down and stopped talking when they saw Thora.

With her wet ponytail falling into her face and her well-worn Halla-Skin still dripping from her swim out to the Rock, Thora *was* a strange sight. She imagined what she must look like to their eyes, and wished she'd taken the time to change and spruce herself up a bit. So much for good impressionistics!

'The matinee doesn't start until one o'clock,' said the tallest and the most serious-looking of the sisters. She had a long nose and wore stylish red-framed glasses like the ones that Thora had seen on the reporters in Milan, after Halla had swum the Rubicon. From what Mr Walters had told her of the sisters, Thora guessed that this one was Lottie.

'She's soaking wet – she's shivering!' said the smallest sister, who must be Dottie.

'Her lips are blue!' said the third, obviously Flossie.

There was no time to waste on chitchat. 'I've come to talk to you about Thor,' said Thora.

Astonished, they all said the name together. 'Thor?'

'He used to work here. Do you remember him?'

'Why?' asked Dottie cagily. 'What do you know of him?'

'Quite a lot, on the one hand. Nothing on the other. I've never met him. He disappeared before I was even born.'

'Is this some sort of hoax?' snapped Lottie, her face stern as a rock sculpture.

'Not that I know of.'

'Who sent you?'

Thora considered their question carefully. 'Nobody. I'm his *daughter*. My name is Thora.'

The sisters looked in the direction of the blackboard, where Kat had written Thora's name.

'My mother told me he once worked here. She told me I should come to you if I got into trouble.'

'Who *is* your mother?' demanded Lottie.

'Halla.'

'Let's go where we can talk,' said Lottie, unlocking the door of the cinema.

Thora followed Lottie and the two other sisters, Dottie and Flossie, down a dark corridor to a fragrant and spacious kitchen with an enormous stove. She felt better immediately. The room was furnished with a table and painted blue chairs, and counter tops cluttered with gleaming saucepans and other cooking utensils. An agile grey cat peered out at Thora then disappeared under the table. There was also an antique-looking high chair that seemed as if it hadn't been used in many, many years. The photos of movie stars that hung on the walls were faint with age. Thora could only just make out the writing.

To Dottie, KEEP SMILING. Clark Gable.

Love you Dottie, don't ever change. Frank S.

Dottie passed Thora a soft fleecy blanket. Once the tea was served, Lottie sat down in front of Thora. She held herself very straight and took a deep breath. 'So,' she said. 'Thor's daughter.'

Thora nodded.

'What sort of age are you?'

'Ten years and one month.'

'Your mother is really Halla?'

Tears welled in Thora's eyes as she thought of her mother. 'Yes.'

Lottie paused for a moment to let Thora collect herself and then continued with her questions. 'How can you prove this?'

Thora pulled off one of her slippers and waggled her toes. The cold had turned her feet and ankles an especially violent shade of purple.

The sisters leaned forward.

Lottie nodded. 'Mermaid.' It was a statement of fact.

Nobody said anything for a moment.

'Well, technically speaking, I am *half*-mermaid,' Thora said. 'As you can see, I don't have a tail.'

Flossie giggled nervously. Dottie began to sob.

'Hush,' said Lottie. 'Do you have any *more* proof?'

Thora pointed to the floor. 'See that little puddle?'

'So *that's* why Kat banished her,' said Dottie.

Thora shrugged, and said, 'Well, my mother *did* tell me humans could be funny about this sort of thing . . .'

She unfastened her ponytail. She had spent so much effort *hiding* her mermaid-ness that it felt strange to be showing it off! And yet it was also a tremendous relief.

It took a few seconds to get her blow hole revved up. The water trickled out in a thin stream.

'My goodness,' said Lottie.

Then *whoosh!* A great torrent of water gushed out as if from a strong garden hose.

Lottie was too startled to duck out of the way. Her glasses flew off her nose and she blinked the water out of her eyes. Her wet hair lay flat on top of her head.

'So it's true!' said Flossie excitedly.

'Oh, I *am* sorry,' said Thora to Lottie. 'I'm a little rusty. It's been ages since I've used my jet stream . . .'

Lottie shook her head. 'Don't worry. I'll dry.'

Dottie now took charge. Her red-rimmed eyes burned into Thora. 'We thought you were a spy for Frooty de Mare. That he'd named you Thora – to echo the name of our own Thor – as part of a cruel joke.'

'Kat reported that while we were away a girl calling herself Thora kept showing up here,' added Flossie. 'She said she'd banished you for spilling your drink but you kept returning anyway. That sort of persistance has a Frooty de Mare quality about it and it set off the alarm bells. We just didn't think that you might be . . .'

The two other sisters suddenly lost all their reserve. Tears now sprang into their eyes as well.

Then Dottie reached out and embraced Thora. She stroked her head. She almost squeezed her half to death!

'. . . My granddaughter.'

Chapter 47

When Thora was small, she had often dreamed of a moment when she would find herself surrounded by family, everybody hugging, crying and saying how much they loved one another.

What she hadn't anticipated was how strange it would be to learn that she had a surname!

Thora *Greenberg*!

As Dottie embraced her, Thora chuckled to herself. No, it was not how she had dreamed it. It was much, much, much *better*! She pinched herself on the arm, so hard that she cried 'Ouch!'

'Why did you do that?' asked Flossie, horrified.

'I want to make sure that this is not just a wonderful dream that I am going to wake up from.'

When long-lost relatives are brought together, they often just like to sit and stare at one another. To bask in each other's gaze the way a fish might linger in a

sunny spot. Dottie, Lottie, Flossie and Thora did just that. They had so much to tell each other and so much to ask that they didn't know where to start. Questions and answers kept dissolving into tears, hugs and laughter. Then Flossie got it into her head that Thora must eat, and so she busied herself with heating up one of her soups. Dottie sat as close as possible to Thora, as if she meant to inhale her. Lottie chattered away about how they had given up hope of ever seeing Thor again, and *now his daughter was seated right before them, sporting eyes the very same colour as Thor's as well as his funny habit of scratching his elbows!*

'He loved Flossie's soups,' said Dottie.

'Especially my turnip soup. Please try it. You look like you need some.' Flossie handed Thora a bowl.

'We hoped to give him the cinema to run as his own.'

'He was the best projectionist in the business,' said Dottie.

'It's all computerised now. We haven't kept up.'

'But your father would have!'

'Such a clever chap!'

'One day he came to work and announced that he had met the woman he wanted to marry.'

'He had caught her in his fishing net.'

'He was smitten.'

'"Head over tails" is how my mother put it,' said Thora between gulps.

'We were very pleased for him. Admittedly, we worried a little when we learned that Halla was a mermaid.'

'Yes,' said Flossie. 'Humans and mermaids are like oil and water.'

'We didn't say that to him, of course.'

'Young people have to find things out for themselves.'

'And he was so happy.'

'He warned us that he had to be very careful. We would have liked a big wedding, but he explained that they would have to get married in secret.'

'We agreed to meet him at the *Loki* the night after the wedding. We wanted to meet his bride and give her a gift. But they never showed up.'

'We went back the next day.'

'And the next.'

'A few months later, the mayor told us that he was sorry, but he had to put the *Loki* up for sale. We were going to buy it, but decided it was too full of sad memories. And none of us knows anything about boats.'

'Then one night, less than a year on, a tall man dressed in white knocked on the window of the cinema.'

'A perfect English gent,' said Flossie.

'Mr Walters!' cried Thora in delight.

'At first we thought it very peculiar.'

'Looking for milk in the middle of the night.'

'But when we learned it was for a hungry baby girl, we let him in.'

'We gave him some baby things. A blanket, a rattle, a milk bottle . . .'

'And a bunny rabbit!' cried Thora excitedly. There was a ripping sound as Thora pulled open one of the Velcro pockets on her Halla-Skin and fished out a piece of old fur for the sisters to inspect. It was neither blue nor yellow, but something in between. 'The rabbit!' she said. 'It's been everywhere with me, even Timbuktu!'

Dottie sighed. 'It was your father's originally.'

Lottie continued with the story. 'Mr Walters came by the next day to thank us. He was just so . . .'

'Dreamy!' exclaimed Flossie.

'That same day, the *Loki* sailed away. We learned he had bought it.'

'He sent Flossie postcards from around the world.'

'From Finland one year, Japan another.'

'One year from Tahiti!'

'He said he was keeping an eye on his fairy godchild and her mother.'

'He never mentioned you or your mother by name. We had no idea.'

'In his last letter, Mr Walters said he would be returning soon,' said Flossie. 'But he was never very specific. Where is he now?'

'He'll turn up soon,' said Thora. 'He always does.'

'And what about your mother?' Lottie asked innocently.

Tears welled in Thora's eyes. The time had come to tell them about her great problem. 'I don't know where she is!'

'You don't *know*?'

'Not for certain. You see, she was living on the Rock, but she's not there any more. I just swam out this morning and couldn't find her. But I'm almost positive that she's been captured – and that Frooty de Mare's going to do something with her at the opening of his new cinema!'

'Frooty!' yelped Flossie. 'That bauble-nosed bandit!'

Dottie glanced at her watch. 'How the time has flown! The cinema opening begins at five ... only a few hours to go.'

Lottie pursed her lips again. 'Well, it certainly

sounds like one of Frooty's cruel pranks. He's been casting about for years to find something that will wipe us off the map. But I reckon he's gone too far this time. What do you think, girls?'

Flossie and Dottie nodded in agreement.

'What should I do?' asked Thora anxiously.

'You must go to the opening of the Mermaid Cinema. We've been banned from attending. When you see your mother, you must pass this on to her,' said Lottie. She took a small square box out of a drawer and passed it to Thora.

'Your mother's wedding gift, which we never had the chance to give her,' said Flossie.

Thora opened the box and removed a gold band. She held it up. 'It's warm,' she said.

'So it should be,' said Lottie. 'It's the projectionist's ring. It was used to filter all the magic of cinema in this theatre from the day we opened to the day your father disappeared. So many hopes and dreams and promises have passed through that ring that it's surprising it's still able to keep its shape.'

Thora turned it round and peered through it at the sisters. 'What will it do?'

'Projectionist's rings are generally magic,' said Lottie. 'They bring good luck. But it really depends on who wears them.'

'Put it on,' urged Lottie. 'If it hums, it's on your side.'

It was too large for Thora's ring finger, so she slipped it on to her thumb. Instantly, she felt a faint vibrating sensation.

'It will help you sort out this business with Frooty. I believe it's helped us deal with him for years.'

The matter-of-fact manner of the sisters reassured Thora no end.

'Now go,' said Dottie, biting her lip to try and stop the tears from welling up in her eyes. 'If only we could go with you!'

Chapter 48

Frooty was rushing about the great foyer of the new Mermaid Cinema when the phone call came.

An English voice said, 'Mr De Mare?'

'Speaking,' said Frooty.

'It's Wally Jack. I'll be there in one hour. Just left the airport.'

'Yippee!' cried Frooty. He grabbed hold of Mrs de Mare and gave her a hug. 'We scored, Tweety Bird!' he exclaimed. 'The great BBC news reporter, Mr Wally Jack, has travelled all the way from *London* to cover our story!'

'Well, I should hope so,' sniffed Mrs de Mare. 'After all, this will be *international news.*'

Chapter 49

Frooty was on top of the world.

All the people who had doubted him and criticised him and even *laughed* at him were now *pouring* into his cinema. All of them stuffing themselves on the free onion rings, popcorn balls and blue licorice bluebottles.

But most satisfying of all, *eating their own words*!

Soon everybody would be milling about in the Sea King Games Room (another unique feature of the Mermaid Cinema), throwing away their money on the slot machines. *Spending, spending, spending!* And just think how they would spend once they saw the main attraction!

There would be busloads of tourists from all over the country.

Chartered jets full of wealthy foreigners with fat wallets.

Frooty grew a little dizzy thinking about it.

He snaked expertly through the crowd, passing balloons to babies, waving modestly to the cameras. He would save his biggest smile for the BBC, for Mr Wally Jack.

This was what he'd *dreamed*!

One day in the not-so-distant future people would begin to appreciate the magnitude of his genius.

His thoughts galloped ahead. He imagined tomorrow's headlines.

FROOTY DE MARE.
CINEMA KING OF
THE 21st CENTURY.

First, Grimli.

Then, the world!

All these twit-brained lumpfish were in for a *big surprise*.

Chapter 50

Outside the Allbent, Thora and Cosmo sat on a bench, still absorbing the conversation with the sisters. On Thora's thumb, the projectionist's ring felt warm. It was a simple band with a delicate serrated edge. She removed it and peered inside. It had been engraved:

TO THE MARRIAGE OF EARTH AND SEA.

'Thor was of the earth and Halla of the sea,' she said to Cosmo. 'That makes me a bit of both.' And with that thought Thora made her way back to the beach and walked along the shore.

Half of the land and sea. Half dry, half wet. Human and mermaid. Thora. Me.

It was Cosmo who broke her reverie. She was startled to see how much time had passed. She refastened her ponytail, and with a surge of purpose she and Cosmo walked from the beach to join the crowd that had gathered around the Mermaid Cinema.

A three-piece Dixieland band had been set up on the front patio of the new building. Thora was disturbed to see that the musicians were dressed up as mermaids, their legs stuffed into long green tails, their hair (most certainly wigs!) tumbling over their shoulders. A lurid neon sign blinked THE MERMAID CINEMA. The licence plate on a long white stretch limousine in front read CINEMA KING.

'It reminds me of the Motel Skwander in Las Vegas,' Thora said to Cosmo. 'The tinfoily effect.'

Cosmo spread his tail and nodded.

They walked past a camera crew and up the stairs into a foyer called The Popcorn Hall. Large banquet tables heaved with food. The air was prickly with onion gas and the slightly eggy stench of not-so-freshly-popped popcorn. Everybody was talking and chewing and swallowing at once.

'Oh, look!' Thora exclaimed to Cosmo. 'It's Mrs Grubb.'

In addition to her silly germ-repelling face mask, Mrs Grubb was wearing green eye shadow and a fluffy pink cardigan.

'Ah,' said Mrs Grubb. 'Surprise, surprise. It's our sickly little orphan girl. Do you realise that what you did to the Rukles when you ran off was not only rude and ungrateful, but also had tragic consequences for the Rukle family?'

'You mean Mr Rukle had no money that night for the slot machines?'

Mr Rukle then appeared at Mrs Grubb's side. 'She made my wife and children leave me. Now I have nothing.' He buried his face in his hands and began to cry.

'See?' said Mrs Grubb. 'Reducing a grown man to tears! What will your next prank be? I am very disappointed in you, Thora. Nobody tried harder than I to help you.'

Mr Rukle stuffed something into his trouser pocket. 'Whaddina dog's breakfast are *you* staring at?' he demanded. The veins in his temples throbbed accusingly.

'I believe you have an allergy to onion rings,' replied Thora. 'Maybe you ought to borrow a pair of my goggles. Mr Walters wears them when he chops onions.'

Mrs Grubb made a *humph* noise. 'I want you to know, little missy, that I am not finished with you yet. Not surprisingly, it's been impossible to find another family who will take you on. But I do not give up easily.'

'Thora doesn't need a foster family,' a voice suddenly quipped. 'She's already got a family of her own.'

It was Holly!

'I would advise you to mind your own business, Miss de Mare,' snapped Mrs Grubb. 'And does your father have any idea who you are consorting with?'

'Frankly, Mrs Grubb, I don't give a damn,' said Holly.

Thora couldn't believe her ears.

Mrs Grubb sputtered. 'Rude girl!'

'Thora is my best friend on earth,' continued Holly, loudly enough to turn heads. 'Next to Lynne and Ricky Rukle, of course. Come on, Thora. Let's get something to eat.'

Holly's words took Thora by surprise. *My best friend on earth!* Nobody her age had ever said such a nice thing about her. The ring on her thumb hummed. How was it that terrible things could happen at the same time as wonderful things? Bad and good together. Life on land was very strange.

At that moment, the Rukle children came bounding toward them.

'Thora!' they cried. 'Are we glad to see you! What did the Greenberg sisters say?'

The children huddled in the corner of the foyer. Thora spoke fast, in a whisper. There was not enough time to tell them everything, but she showed them the ring on her thumb and let them feel the magical warmth it emanated.

Ricky leaned forward and impulsively planted a kiss on Thora's cold cheek. Thora felt that same mysterious heat rising on her face.

The crackle of a microphone put an end to the pleasant interlude. They each grabbed a bucket of popcorn balls and went to join the crowd.

Chapter 51

From a platform at the back of the cinema foyer, Frooty fiddled with the microphone. 'Ladies and gentlemen, boys and girls, while we wait for Mr Wally Jack, the great foreign news reporter from London, I would like to welcome you all to the great Mermaid Cinema.'

He pointed to a large screen on the wall behind him. 'Let me draw your attention to all the wonderful new features of this great modern cinema. Unlike the Allbent, this building was built especially to show you the latest films from Hollywood. It features three viewing theatres with snazzy red velvet seats.'

'We peeked inside,' whispered Lynne. 'The theatres are so small they'll give everyone claustrophobia. They'll have to squish in like sardines!'

'And the seats are *fake* velvet,' added Ricky.

Frooty continued. 'In keeping with my interest in

aquatic motifs, neon lighting experts have created these visually stunning displays of marine life for you to enjoy while you queue to see your film. In no other cinema in the world can you see such original use of neon! Oh, and the snack bar will offer you an astonishing range of treats: popcorn of course, but also fish-shaped drops, butter-mallow squid, chocolate starfish and our very own jellied mermaids – invented by our resident sweets expert Mr Siegfried Twizzle!'

There was a burst of applause for a roly-poly man in a white tuxedo.

'Now, Mr Wally Jack will be here any minute. But let us delay no further. This is the moment you have all been waiting for. *The Big Surprise*. Let us all stand back a little to make room. Any pushing or shoving and you will be asked to leave.'

Thora and her friends exchanged glances.

Suddenly, there came a great creaking, squeaking, splashing sound.

Six people – including Madge, wearing a sparkly green top adorned with a cardboard dorsal fin – were rolling into the main foyer what appeared to be an enormous rectangular box on wheels. It was the size of a moving truck and was covered with red and white striped wrapping paper. A large pink bow sat on the top.

Everyone whispered at once.

Thora felt her heart sink.

Up on the podium, Frooty de Mare looked very happy. Mrs de Mare also looked very happy. They seemed to grow taller, wider and happier as they surveyed the crowd.

'Ladies and gentlemen,' said Frooty, 'I am not a poet, darn it. I wish I were. Like you, I am a simple man. A man with a dream.'

He dabbed his eye with a handkerchief.

Thora wondered if he was using an onion to make his tears too.

'May I invite my daughter and her little friends to step forward and remove the wrapping paper?' He flashed them a piratical grin.

Holly, Thora, Lynne and Ricky joined hands and stepped forward.

Thora was the tallest. With a heavy heart she reached up and took hold of the bow. She pulled.

There was a ripping sound. She looked around.

'Now, wait a minute,' said Frooty.

The crowd urged her on. The room pulsed with curiosity. Everyone was desperate to know. *What was it?*

Thora continued pulling and ripping. In the strip where the paper had been removed, glass.

'An aquarium?' guessed Ricky.

Now all the children grabbed handfuls of paper. They tore and they ripped. Soon the floor was a sea of red and white paper, a little like a scene of Christmas morning on a Swiss Christmas card.

Though of course, mermaids don't celebrate Christmas.

A thick silence fell.

'Wow!' said Mr Rukle.

Dimly, Thora registered the roar of astonishment and excitement. People were clapping. Talking. Corks popped and outside firecrackers sizzled in the sky.

WHIZZZZ. BOOOM. WHIZZZZA. KABOOOM.

Thora felt as if she were swimming through cotton wool.

She stepped up close and pressed her face against the cold glass.

'Oh, Mother,' she whispered. 'It really is you.'

Chapter 52

Halla looked terrible.

Topped with a plastic tiara, her beautiful blonde hair had been sprayed with glitter and her tail had lost its shimmer.

It was as if she'd been beached and bleached – which, as she would later tell Thora and Mr Walters, was pretty much what happened when she was captured by Frooty and the coast guard and hauled over to the Mermaid Cinema to be displayed in a tank of polluted water.

'How awful ... how terrible,' said Holly. 'Even worse than I imagined.'

'Oh, Thora!' cried Lynne. 'Your poor mother!'

'We've got to get her out,' said Ricky with determination.

Frooty's voice boomed over the loudspeaker. 'OK, tweety birds, let's move back from the aquarium. Let

everyone get a view. Only fair!'

Thora tried to climb into the tank. 'Help me!' she cried to the others.

'Get down!' ordered Frooty. 'Step aside! Let the journalists in with their cameras. Do you hear me?'

Holly, Ricky and Lynne tried to lift Thora. She reached up to the top of the tank but couldn't get a grip. Some sort of plastic screen was acting as a lid and there was nowhere to get a foothold on the slippery glass. She slid back down.

A photographer from the *Daily Seasider* began to shout. 'Get those brats out of the way! I don't have all day!'

People swarmed around.

Halla tried to leap up the side of the tank, but she was too weak. She swam in confused circles in the murky water.

Thora could see that her mother was very ill. She'd seen her like this twice before: once while on tour in Alaska in the freezing cold, and another time after swimming in the filthy Danube River near the Hungarian border, when her tail became fouled with oil. Perhaps the water in the tank was not even salt water!

Mother and daughter stared helplessly at each other. Halla had never looked so sad. Were those tears? Was the water level rising?

But mermaids didn't cry.

It was a fact.

So what was this?

'Any minute now, folks ... the great BBC news man will be here!'

'A world exclusive!' shouted Mrs de Mare.

'Stand back, everybody!'

'He's here. Hurrah!'

'Mr Wally Jack!'

Thora felt Frooty's hands on her shoulders.

'Move on. Let the reporter through.'

Thora tried to wriggle away, when she noticed that the ring on her thumb was vibrating, growing lighter in colour and warmer by the second. Now it seemed to be boiling with anger. It was how *she* felt too!

She slipped the ring off her thumb and passed it to Holly. 'Put it on Cosmo's beak!' she whispered.

Without the ring on her thumb, Frooty was stronger than anything she'd ever encountered. He was hauling her away. Through the crowd, she saw Holly stepping up to Cosmo to fit the ring on his beak as Thora had asked.

'Use your beak, Cosmo!' Thora hollered. 'Use your beak!'

Frooty dumped Thora into the cinema kitchen and slammed the door.

'Ow!' she cried, landing heavily against a huge industrial popcorn machine. 'I've burned myself!'

She examined her hand, but it was not burned at all.

On her thumb was a mark left by the projectionist's ring.

With renewed strength, she jumped up and pushed open the blocked door. It was as if another hand were helping her. To her surprise, it opened.

She was just in time to see a tall man dressed in white weaving his way through the crowd. Not as agile as he'd once been, but with a stride that was determined and confident.

He wore a lettuce-green fedora on his head. A camera was slung at a jaunty angle over his shoulder.

'Mr Wally Jack!' said Frooty, immensely relieved.

Thora smiled over the mix-up. Boy, was Frooty in for a big surprise!

The crowd parted to let Mr Walters through.

Frooty rushed back to the podium. 'Welcome, Mr Jack!' he said, and handed him the microphone.

Mr Walters nodded. He regarded the crowd with his rather popping blue eyes. 'This place that Frooty de Mare has called the Mermaid Cinema is a truly vile establishment,' he announced.

His voice had all the authority of a veteran newsman.

A surprised hush fell over the room. Frooty's mouth hung open.

'Cosmo? Didn't you hear what Thora said? Use your beak, bird!' Mr Walters commanded.

Cosmo stood tall before the aquarium. Almost a metre in height.

He puffed out his chest, spread his tail, drew back his aristocratic head and then, with one hard forward rap, dashed his beak against the glass.

Chapter 53

Even the Greenberg sisters heard the CRACK.

The unmistakable sound of an aquarium splitting down the middle. With slightly trembling hands, Lottie passed Flossie her opera glasses and urged her to take a look.

They were really too old to be sitting on the roof.

What if one of them fell off?

But when the call had come in from Mr Walters that afternoon, shortly after Thora's visit, they'd donned their warm pink tracksuits and packed a picnic basket with a Thermos of hot chocolate, three tin cups, muesli bars, a stopwatch, blankets, hats and a Polaroid camera. Then they'd closed the cinema until further notice and climbed up on to its sloping tiled roof to watch and wait.

Over the telephone Mr Walters hadn't been able to say for sure how it would all turn out, but he had promised them a show they would never forget.

They hadn't been disappointed.

'Life really is so much more *thrilling* than fiction,' Dottie would reflect later. Even though Lottie considered such statements to be worn-out clichés (especially as her sister had got the phrase wrong), she had to admit that what they'd witnessed was as good as any of the movies that had flickered across their dusty old screen for some thirty years.

At approximately seven in the evening, Mr Walters had cantered up to the entrance of the Mermaid Cinema on a magnificent horse, followed on foot by an irate policeman in a red tunic with shiny gold buttons.

Mr Walters had proffered the sisters a discreet wave. His eyes had lingered a little longer on Flossie than the other two – though he hadn't been so corny as to wink or blow a kiss, as Flossie secretly wished he had.

They'd watched him dismount ('So spry for a man his age!' sighed Flossie) and bound up the stairs. In his youth he'd been a dashing sportsman, coach and journalist. In middle age, he'd commanded vast radio audiences with his deep, clean-cut enunciation and crisp diction. And now, in his dramatic return to Grimli, he seemed to display each and every one of the qualities that had been required of him in those demanding professions.

According to Dottie's stopwatch, Mr Walters had been inside the Mermaid Cinema for three minutes and twenty-four seconds when the sound of cracking glass reached them.

After four minutes and thirteen seconds, water began to trickle out the front doors of the cinema.

Through a shared lens, the sisters watched the trickle grow to a powerful stream.

The stream to a river.

The river coursed out of the front door and down the steps.

They could not hear anyone screaming in fright, because it was not really very frightening. The river was well behaved. It formed a sort of elegant pathway leading out of the building. It flowed with the sort of control you associate with rivers that are banked on both sides. It was a friendly sort of river that made you want to jump in for a swim.

Then all three sisters saw them.

Almost directly underneath the Allbent Cinema, Thora was waving and grinning widely as if she were doing nothing more unusual than riding in a festival float in a town parade. Halla looked up and smiled too.

'So *that's* who Thor married.'

'Finally we meet her!'

'She looks like a very nice mermaid.'

'Doesn't she?'

'Now, get back from the edge, Dottie.'

They watched as the water carried Thora and Halla past the fish shop, the bakery, the hardware store and down along the Grimli pier. And hurrying it along while at the same time pointing the way was a rather friendly breeze, whose modest goal seemed simply, as Lottie later put it, to deliver mother and daughter out of harm's way.

Yes, a sensitive breeze, sighed Flossie, that guided the flow of water around the old red oil drum at the end of the pier ('It could have just knocked it over, after all!') before finally, gently, sweetly and carefully, like a giant's hand, releasing mother and daughter safely into the calm of the sea.

The *Loki*
Somewhere in the
Indian Ocean
40 degrees S
60 degrees E
Speed: 8 knots per hour

Dearest Holly,

How are you, my great and worthy amigo? I hope this
finds you hale and hearty as an Olympic hammer
thrower. We have been sailing hard for three weeks
now and we think we've outwitted the coast guard.
After Cosmo cracked the aquarium with the help of
the projectionist's ring, we boarded a magic carpet
of water that took us all the way to the Rock. We did
not have to wait long before we heard, on a
megaphone, Mr Walters' heart-warming 'Ahoy!' He
lost his fedora in all the excitement, which is a
shame because it was brand new. And poor Cosmo lost
some of his prized eye feathers, which will take a
long time to grow back. That night, he drowned his
sorrows in a bottle of raspberry cordial and then he
got very seasick. I don't expect he'll be up to
delivering this letter to you. I may have to ask

the hungry-looking gull who has been trailing us since we left Grimli.

Our plans are still a little up in the air, so I am not sure when we will see you again. You were such a help, 'like a warming drop of Scotch whisky in the heart', as Mr Walters said. I get goosebumps remembering your words. Perhaps that is what having a best friend is meant to feel like. I have told my mother everything about you. She says you sound *lovely* and she wants you to know that the mermaid who visited us that night on the boat was *her* best friend, Marina, and you are not to worry about her, because she is safe as a clam on the ocean floor. Mother thinks you were very brave to place the ring on Cosmo's beak. She asks me to pass on her deepest phosphorescence.

Although I am sad that we have parted, there is a ray of sunshine too. I am glad that nobody will be trying to make me go to school, or join a frosted family, or any of that other malarkey.

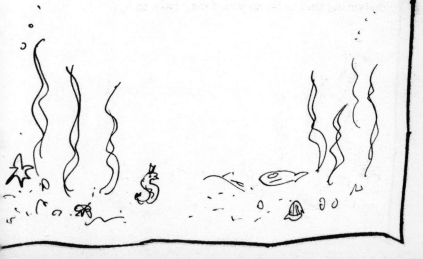

I hope the lunkheads are treating you well. I am
enclosing some tips I picked up from Boris the
Remarkable, just in case you need to un-hypnotise
them.

It is very delicious to be reunited with my mother.
I do not yet know all the glory details about her
capture. She is not the sort of mermaid who likes to
dwell in dark pools. But I am returning with this
letter three of the six teeth your father lost in his
struggle to capture her. My mother has scrubbed
them up with a pumice stone and polished them with
swordfish oil. You can imagine our surprise when we
discovered that they are actually made of gold!
Though she does not yet have her shimmer back, she
is now in good spirits. She is reading a book about
the wind. She just told me that the word 'cloud' is
from the Greek word for 'buttocks'! She doesn't have
buttocks and so she didn't understand why Mr
Walters turned red and had to leave the room when we
started to examine the clouds overhead.

So long, my far-flung best friend. Please give my warmest regards to my good mates Ricky and Lynne. I am sure that if Lynne is willing to be shot out of cannons, she will some day make it to the Moscow Circus (though I think I would prefer it if she learned the art of contortion – much less noisy and not as apt to scare Cosmo). Some day I hope to meet up again with Ricky. Please don't tell a soul, old soul, but he said he'd like to take me to the Rock and kiss me again! (I still think that swimming with dolphins in Zanzibar would be more fun.)

Farewell!

Write if you remember!

Thora Greenberg

Your best friend.

XXXXX

P.S. Please, I beg you never to mention that part about Ricky. It is most definitely highly calcified information!

Continued in "Thora and the Green Sea-Unicorn"

Gillian Johnson grew up in Winnipeg, where she spent her winters speed-skating at the Sargent Park Oval and her summers swimming in Lake Winnipeg. She now lives in England and Tasmania with her husband, writer Nicholas Shakespeare, and their two sons, Max and Benedict.

More Thora from Hodder Children's Books:

THORA AND THE GREEN SEA-UNICORN

Gillian Johnson

Thora sails to London with Halla, Cosmo, Mr Walters – and her newest friend, Shirley the sea-unicorn.

In London, Thora encounters the washed-up actress Pamela P. Poutine, a mermaid Cruella de Vil who makes her living selling tropical fish. It doesn't take long for Pamela to go after the rare and priceless green sea-unicorn. When the theft goes wrong, she sets her sights on Thora's magical projectionist's ring . . .